PRAISE FOR

IN SIGHT OF THE MOUNTAIN

"Anna's struggle to find her place in a society that wants to constrain her within appropriate gender roles is enhanced by the author's attention to details—of fashion, culture, and even mountain climbing. **An engaging escapade with a feisty female lead**."
—*Kirkus Reviews*

"Searching for purpose and adventure, Anna will win your heart over and then some. Filled with lessons of strength, perseverance, and audacity, In Sight of the Mountain is a beautifully written story. **A must-read** for those who are striving to fulfill their dreams."
—Kristi Elizabeth, *Seattle Book Review*

"Focusing on themes of the liberation of women, the American class system and effects of colonialism, this intelligent and heart-warming novel introduces us to Anna Gallagher at the tender age of nineteen. . . **An epic and gripping work of historical fiction**. . . Overall, In Sight of the Mountain is the perfect historical read for fans of pioneering heroes and tales of triumph over discrimination."
—K.C. Finn, *Reader's Favorite* (5 Star Review)

IN LIGHT OF THE SUMMIT

The Rainier Series, Book 2

JAMIE MCGILLEN

Foreword by
CHARLOTTE AUSTIN

ALSO BY JAMIE MCGILLEN

In Sight of the Mountain

THE SEQUEL TO IN SIGHT OF THE MOUNTAIN

IN LIGHT

OF THE

SUMMIT

JAMIE MCGILLEN

Special discounts for bulk purchases
for book clubs can be requested by
contacting the author directly at
jamie@jamiemcgillen.com.
She loves book clubs.
Like, seriously loves them.

COVER DESIGN BY ANA GRIGORIU-VOICU
AUTHOR PHOTO BY MELISSA NOLEN
MAP DESIGN BY ZENTA BRICE

Library Cataloging-in-Publication Data

1. Young Women—Fiction. 2. Women mountaineers—Washington (State)—
Fiction. 3. Washington (State)—History—Fiction. 4. Rainier, Mount (Wash.)
—Fiction. 5. United States—Social conditions—19th century—Fiction.

ISBN 978-1-7334239-5-3 (paperback)
ISBN 978-1-7334239-1-5 (ebook)

First Edition

For my honeymooner, Kyle.
You're my favorite.

He soon felt that the fulfillment of his desires gave him only one grain of the mountain of happiness he had expected. This fulfillment showed him the eternal error men make in imagining that their happiness depends on the realization of their desires.

—Leo Tolstoy, from *Anna Karenina*

Out of the forest at last, there stood the mountain, wholly unveiled, awful in bulk and majesty, filling all the view like a separate newborn world.

—John Muir, from "An Ascent of Mount Rainier"

CONTENTS

FOREWORD

BY CHARLOTTE AUSTIN

Climbing mountains, largely speaking, is rarely straight-forward. Routes twist and bend, at times leading to false summits. Maps, if they exist, may be vague. Some footholds are secure; others, seemingly identical, crumble into powder at the gentlest touch. Rain or snow is almost guaranteed. Crevasses can appear from nowhere, blocking the path. And with each step into these winding alpine labyrinths, every climber digs deeply within themselves. Each footstep is a gamble, an act of faith, a prayer.

In Jamie McGillen's delightful first novel, *In Sight of the Mountain*, we followed the story of an ambitious young woman's pursuit of her dream to climb Mount Rainier. Set in the Pacific Northwest more than a hundred years ago, Anna's story is still relatable today: after years of seeing the tallest mountain in Washington state loom on the horizon over Seattle for most of her young life, she decides to try to reach the summit. Our heroine trains, gathers her resources, and pieces together the best gear she can manage to find. Ultimately, while she learns tremendous lessons on the mountain's spectacular flanks, she does not reach the summit — but she does descend safely, with dignity and grace. She returns home to her family with sore feet, but she is wiser, more humble, and more determined than ever to find a path toward touching the sky.

In this book, *In Light of the Summit*, Anna is still spunky — but she's also older, wiser, and more mountain-savvy. Her training is more calculated; she assesses her gear with a veteran's eye; and she approaches her return to Mount Rainier with that delicate balance found only in experienced climbers: she is somehow simultaneously more confident and more humble. It's beautiful. It's relatable. It's realistic. And in the way that sometimes only novels can be, it's ultimately more true. I couldn't help but cheer for her with every turn of the page, and I have no doubt that you'll do the same.

There's more to this book than Anna's ultimate success, however. In more than a decade of climbing mountains professionally, I've struggled with many of the climbing-related challenges described in these books: sexism, self-doubt, family complications, social pressure, even the difficulties of finding boots that properly fit. I spent most of my twenties as a climbing guide on Mount Rainier, and I've spent hundreds — probably approaching thousands — of days on those blue-gray glaciers, learning many of the same lessons described in these books. Recently I've spent more of my time climbing and guiding internationally on peaks including Denali (20,308ʹ), Mount Elbrus (18,510ʹ), and Mount Everest (29,029ʹ), but I'll never forget the tenacity, perseverance, and perspective I gleaned while exploring my home state's tallest peak.

It's incredibly rare to see those lessons reflected in modern-day literature, and it's for that reason that I'm so excited to see this wonderful author continue this remarkable story. Despite the leaps and bounds we have achieved in the last century, women are still the overwhelming minority in the realms of alpinism and mountaineering — and I believe that's largely due to lack of representation in popular media, in folklore, and in the stories we tell. When our children are brought up hearing tales of adventure by all genders, I'll rest easily — but until then, I'll be working hard to support and uplift the incredibly important work of authors who, like Jamie McGillen, are sharing stories of women in the alpine.

In 1984, Rosie Andrews wrote that most male climbers raised in traditional Western culture have "generally been encouraged to perform physically, problem-solve, and take risks while [...] girls are usually more sheltered and protected. Rather than being prepared for independence, [women] learn to expect to play a supporting role, which hinges upon reliance on others." Recent gender studies expand on this idea. In a widely read 2014 *Atlantic* article "The Confidence Gap," Katty Kay and Claire Shipman concluded, after reviewing the research: "Do men doubt themselves? Of course. But not with such exacting and repetitive zeal [as women], and they don't let their doubts stop them as often as women do."

It's not hard to imagine the effects of that confidence (or lack thereof) during bold climbs — and in life. Anna's story is a beautiful, relatable, stand-alone example of a woman who does hard things, and I'm here to cheer her on: for my own sake, for the sake of women everywhere, and for the young people who are learning from the examples we set. Anna's story, while fictional, is important. It's fun. It's entertaining. And it's like nothing else I've ever read.

When I first interacted with Jamie McGillen's writing, I was shocked at the accuracy and insight in her storytelling. Anna's adventures are fun, engrossing, and a page-turning delight. The details are accurate and memorable, the characters are the friends I've always wanted. The love interests are heartwarming, and the dilemmas feel real. But more than that, this narrative is unique. And I couldn't be more excited for you, dear reader, to embark on this new adventure.

—Charlotte Austin
charlotteaustin.com

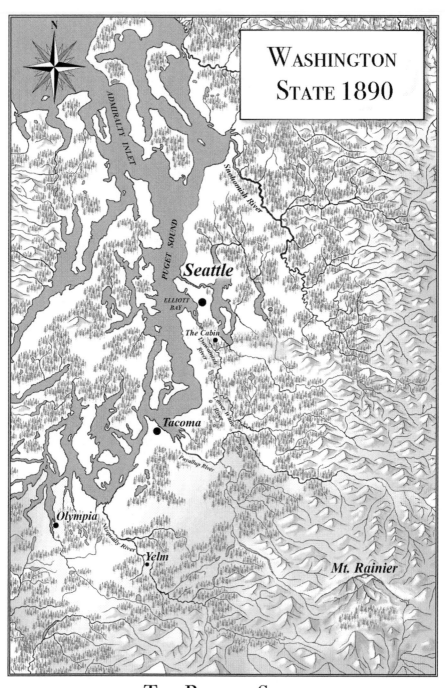

WASHINGTON
STATE 1890

N

ADMIRALTY INLET

Snohomish River

PUGET SOUND

Seattle

ELLIOTT
BAY

The Cabin

Duwamish
River

Green White

Tacoma

Puyallup River

Olympia

Nisqually River

Yelm

Mt. Rainier

IN SIGHT OF THE MOUNTAIN THE RAINIER SERIES IN LIGHT OF THE SUMMIT

CHAPTER ONE

THE ARTICLE

Anna | *October 1890*

Anna Gallagher jumped at the sound of glass shattering. She stood behind the bookstore counter a few feet from where the brick now lay on the floor. Sparkling pieces of broken window covered the tightly knit rug.

"You're the woman who tried to summit the mountain, aren't ya?"

A tall, poorly-dressed man stood outside looking through the jagged opening where the pane had been. She tried to place him but was sure she'd never seen him before. The fire in his eyes made him look as if he might slither through the smashed opening to attack her.

She glanced sideways at her grandfather who had moved forward, both hands raised as if to ask the man to calm down.

"What's the meaning of this?" he asked.

The man pointed up toward the painted sign on the awning that said *Gallagher Bookstore.*

"Are you the one from the newspaper article?"

She glared at him despite the wave of fear that made her legs weak. "Yes, I am."

"Thought so," he said, spitting a giant wad onto the sidewalk. "Women belong at home. Shame on you!"

He turned abruptly and hurried down the street, disappearing into an alleyway between two stone buildings.

She stepped out from behind the counter and shook her head. "John must have written an article for the *Seattle Post-Intelligencer.*"

"What in the world does climbing a mountain have to do with a bookstore?" her grandfather asked lightheartedly, a smile playing on his lips. But as soon as he saw her solemn face, he frowned. "It's nonsense. He's a fool, and our books are too good for a simple man like that. Anyway, it's only one man."

She worked through the scene in her mind, trying not to let it spiral.

One man. Would there be more like him?

Of course there would.

Ever since she'd begun planning her secret escape to climb Mount Rainier, she'd known the stakes were high and that she might never be accepted by some people in Seattle society again. Yet she hadn't planned on it affecting her family's business. How could she have overlooked that?

Tears welled in her eyes, but she blinked them away before turning to her grandfather. "I'm so sorry——"

"I won't hear of it, lassie," he said soothingly, closing the front door with a soft click. "Times are changing, and we all need to move along with them. If an old man like me can learn to accept it, then so can he, eh?"

Anna nodded, but her stomach clenched with the familiar

heaviness of something she couldn't control yet needed to bear.

"I think I'll head home to help Greta with supper," she said quietly.

"Quite right. The day is nearly done. I'll get this all cleaned up."

He put a soft hand on her back, and the warm, gentle touch proved reassuring. Her heartbeat calmed, and the muscles in her shoulders relaxed. He smelled of cinnamon and pine, scents that had always soothed her for as long as she could remember. She released an anxious breath. When she was with her grandfather, the world seemed easier to endure.

She tip-toed carefully around the glass shards on the ground, lifting her skirts with both hands. Thank goodness the soft leather of her boots protected her feet.

As she stepped out the door, she glanced toward the alleyway the angry man had disappeared in, then set out in the opposite direction.

She wrapped her lavender shawl around her shoulders tightly. The soft fabric on her neck provided a welcome sensation—warm and soothing. It protected her from the crisp October wind that swirled around her, blowing golden leaves off the trees that lined the street.

So many of the surrounding downtown buildings were now made of stone, a response to the Great Seattle Fire that had devastated the city just over a year prior.

Part of her wanted to stop at the Yesler Mill to tell Ben what had happened, but no harm had come to her. And he'd be at her house first thing in the morning as he always was on Saturdays. It wouldn't do to interrupt his workday with something that couldn't be helped.

As she passed the tall brick buildings that made up this

new version of the city, an ominous numbness settled in her chest—something uncomfortably cold that she couldn't quite put her finger on. Why should she even care if *one* man had a little fit about her attempt to summit? Others might think differently.

On the wood-planked walkway, she stepped lightly in her black leather shoes on the creaking boards. The smell of sawdust and saltwater surrounded her, and a vivid memory of the angry man yelling at her to stay home brought a wave of nausea. The crazy gleam in his eyes stayed with her even when she closed hers for a respite as she waited for a carriage to pass in front of her.

With the downtown buildings around her, the mountain was out of sight. It had become her rock, her anchor, her port of call in every storm. For so long, she had charted her life around it and the prospect of climbing its slopes.

Not seeing it now made her feel disoriented—lost in a city where men could hurl bricks and insults with no consequences. It made the hair on her arms stand up.

CHAPTER TWO
A SIMPLE LETTER

ANNA

Before the sun rose the next morning, Anna curled up on a wooden chair in front of the fireplace. Esther, the cat, wandered slowly toward her and then leapt onto her lap, plopping down happily under her hand. She had been reading the copy of *Anna Karenina* that Ben had given her when he'd proposed to her. There had been lots of romance, which proved a lovely distraction.

Her favorite line so far was:

He stepped down, trying not to look long at her, as if she were the sun, yet he saw her, like the sun, even without looking.

She wondered if Ben had felt that way when he first met her. The possibility made her smile.

The two months since her attempted summit of Mount

Rainier and his unexpected proposal had been a whirlwind of excitement. Her good friend June was off to California with Connor and their baby, so she visited Heather more often and had even called on Emily a few times. But when she wasn't working at the bookstore, she spent time with Ben.

She had been attempting to convince him to invite his parents to their wedding, but he was hesitant. His relationship with them was more complicated than she had initially thought. Even so, it seemed a shame for them not to reconcile before their union. If only he'd be more willing to open up about his reluctance, perhaps she'd be able to help. Maybe a simple letter and invitation would be all that was needed for them to take the first train from California.

It wouldn't do for her to send the letter herself without Ben's knowledge. Their marriage ought to start with perfect honesty. But she had a sinking feeling he would regret not inviting them. Perhaps his choice was made out of fear and not of a sound mind.

Outside the living room window, slate clouds floated against a light purple sky, and a flock of crows passed by in perfect formation. When she looked back into the room, her grandfather wordlessly joined her by the fire and handed her a mug of coffee.

The warmth settled her, and she thanked her grandfather with a nod and a smile.

While he opened the newspaper, her attention came to rest on her plans to climb the mountain with Ben and the same mountaineering team she'd now grown fond of. With all the rigorous training they planned to do in the meantime, she suspected it would be a much more enjoyable ascent. And this time she might have the honor of summiting.

Because it truly would be an honor—a combination of preparation, fair weather, and a dash of good luck. All the planning in the world couldn't guarantee a successful summit. She knew that now.

It would be a delight to simply share the experience of climbing the mountain with Ben—the wildflowers, deep blue glaciers, the purest air, and breathtaking views. But what a joy it would be if her dreams of summiting came to fruition this time.

"This is a remarkable article, lassie. I'm proud of you," her grandfather said, breaking the silence. Then he settled back into reading the paper with a thoughtful expression.

The thickness in his voice told her he still felt ashamed for how he'd treated her before she'd left for the trip.

Greta emerged from the kitchen, her pink dress swishing around her ankles as she stopped to lean against the frame of the door. "Ben's comin' up the road."

Her grandfather looked up from his newspaper and uncrossed his ankles. "Of course he is. The sun has risen, hasn't it?" He roared with laughter.

Greta rolled her eyes with a half-smile, wiped her hands on the kitchen towel tucked into her white apron, and walked back into the kitchen.

The love Anna felt for Greta had only grown over the last few months. When the older woman had first married Anna's grandfather, she hadn't been so sure about her, but now she was a vital piece of the patchwork family they'd built.

Lifting Esther out of her lap, she stood and plopped the cat onto her grandfather's knees. Thinking of Ben, her stomach squeezed and a grin spread across her face. She threw the front door open, and the crisp fall air blew in through the opening as she flew down the porch stairs to meet him on the road.

He wore a charcoal gray coat that made his tall frame seem even larger, and his bright white smile made her knees weak. He had a newspaper tucked under his arm and when he took off his hat, dark brown hair came tumbling down to brush his ears. He thrust the paper into her hands and gave her a swift kiss on the cheek.

"Have you seen it?" he asked breathlessly. "Did Oscar show you?"

Anna sighed. "I haven't read it yet, but I heard about it."

"What's wrong?" Ben wrapped an arm around her waist. "Look. Here's your name listed among the mountaineering party."

The not-so-distant memory of hawks gliding by as she looked down on the vast green and brown that painted the landscape below crowded her mind. Her heart swelled with pride and longing to be there again, and hopefully to summit and practically enter that beautiful piece of the sky.

Looking down at the article for the first time, she asked, "Does it mention that I failed to summit with the team?"

Ben's lips twisted into a lopsided frown. "The reporter says you were a sterling teammate and allowed the rest of the crew to summit despite an unexpected injury. It must be that redheaded fellow you told us about. The one with glasses."

She nodded silently and read a snippet of the article.

In August of 1890, the Flannaghan mountaineering team summited Mount Rainier. They were accompanied by Miss Anna Gallagher of Seattle, who was unable to summit due to injury, but she was said to be a sterling teammate and allowed the rest of the crew to summit despite the unexpected injury. Even still, she was bested by Miss Fay Fuller of Yelm, who was the first woman to summit Mount Rainier just days after the Flannaghan team's return to base camp.

Anna smiled at the mention of Fay. She'd spent some time with her at base camp, and the woman was truly a delight. A school teacher and journalist, she was the same age as Anna— twenty years old. She hoped to see her again one day.

But then she frowned and handed the paper to Ben. "There was an incident at the bookstore yesterday afternoon."

"What happened?" He put his hand on her lower back, guiding her inside the house, where the warmth proved a welcome respite from the chilly wind.

She explained as best she could in a way she hoped wouldn't make him too worried, but his eyes narrowed.

"Did you recognize the man? What did he look like?"

"No, and don't try to find him either," she said, tilting her head in plea.

He scowled and exhaled loudly. "Well, I'll help with the clean-up at least."

"Already finished," her grandfather said, joining them at the front door. "It's all behind us now."

With a doubtful expression, Ben looked to the older man who nodded once. An understanding seemed to pass between the two of them.

Anna wrung her hands uncomfortably and sat at the dining room table.

Her grandfather sat down next to her. "I know it was only a few months ago that I shared some of the same sentiments as that man, and I'm sorry. I've had so much to dwell on lately, and I hope to be a better man moving forward."

She couldn't help but smile. He'd come a long way in the past year, both in accepting her for who she was—an adventurous risk-taker—but also learning to accept others who were different from him and forgiving himself in the process.

"Still, I wish it didn't affect you, Grandfather."

She turned to Greta. "And I hope it doesn't make business decline."

"We'll manage fine," Greta said. "Like we always have."

"Yes, let's not worry about it." Ben squeezed her hand and pressed his lips together. "Let's talk of something else. Like the fact that I still don't understand why we can't get married right away."

Anna grinned. "Greta says a proper wedding will take at least two months to plan. And I sure love the idea of a Christmastime wedding. It's already October now, so that's not a terribly long wait. Is it?"

The answer was written on his face—a slight torment. The same tightness squeezed her chest whenever he left in the evenings to sleep in the house he'd built for both of them.

"Anything for you, my dear," he said. "The great Saint Nicholas can officiate himself, if you like. Shall I rent a team of dogs to take us north?"

Anna rolled her eyes and shoved off from his arm with a playful grin. "Oh hush. I can't imagine anything more magical than a wedding surrounded by evergreen trees, holly, and a light dusting of snow."

"You mean a light dusting of powdered sugar on the chocolate crinkles," he said, grabbing her hand and pulling her back to his side.

Laughter burst from her belly in a joyful rush. She simply felt so much happiness when he was around. Would that last forever?

He glanced at her with one eyebrow raised in a dramatic fashion. "Of course, it could just as likely rain on our December wedding day. Would that ruin it for you?"

"Not in the slightest," she replied, and she truly meant it. "Grandfather won't quit chanting, *When December's rains fall fast, marry and true love will last.*"

Ben gave her an amused grin.

"It's true!" her grandfather said with enthusiasm.

He had strong superstitions that she didn't really subscribe to, but she wanted a Christmastime wedding anyway, so it all came together nicely. He had also put in a special order for small bells to be handed out to wedding guests to chime as she and Ben walked down the aisle as a married couple. Something about good luck, and also because they wouldn't be able to find the traditional Bells of Ireland flowers in December.

"Do eggs and pancakes sound all right for breakfast?" Greta asked.

Anna moved toward the kitchen and gave her a smile. "I'll start mixing the batter and make more coffee."

"Well, I'll sure miss having the kitchen help when you move out." Greta sighed and paused to roll up the sleeves on her dress. "You'll both come to visit often though. Won't you?"

"Absolutely," Ben replied. "It's nice to have family close by. And one I enjoy being around."

Anna bit her lip, looking down at her fingernails. She was ecstatic that Ben loved her family, but as an orphan herself, she couldn't imagine spending an entire adulthood without parents by choice. He had left on bad terms. That was true. And they had not been the most loving caregivers when he was a child, but perhaps there was more to it than that.

Once in the kitchen, she looked out the window toward the

mountain. It seemed crystal clear from their place, and the sight usually made her vibrate with life. But this time, seeing it made her think of the brick and shards of glass, which cast a pall of darkness over her mood. The repercussions of the article might just be starting.

After making more coffee and mixing the batter for the pancakes, she swooped back into the dining room with a platter of coffee cups and a steaming pitcher.

"How is the committee going for opening up the library, Oscar?" Ben asked.

"The Seattle Public Library should be up and running sometime this spring," her grandfather replied triumphantly. "It's finally considered an official city department, and we should be receiving ten percent of city funds. Well, from what is raised from licenses and fines."

He turned to Anna. "There's a whole group of ladies doing fundraising if you're interested."

"I'm not sure if books and a library full of them would be an interesting enough topic of conversation for Anna," Ben said with a wink.

Her grandfather chuckled. "It's settled then. I'll speak with the committee this week. I'd like my family to have a part in this historic time."

"Sit down, my love," Ben said, standing. "I'll help Greta bring out the food."

The familiar warmth of his attentiveness filled Anna to her toes, and she kissed his cheek before settling down across from her grandfather.

"And how are plans going for the future Chambers mountaineering adventure?" he asked with a twinkle in his eye.

Since the moment she had returned from her climb in

August, she'd been dreaming of returning—to hopefully accomplish what she knew she could. And this time she would get to do it with Ben.

"Coming along nicely," she replied, pouring herself a second cup of coffee. "We should have mostly the same team. Adding Ben, of course. He's already purchased the supplies he didn't have. And I've gotten a pair of boots that fit me fine."

She flushed thinking of the damage done to her feet by her ill-fitting boots in the last attempt. Not only had they rubbed her skin absolutely raw, but they had ultimately caused the injury that prevented her from staying with the team for their summit.

"Very good," her grandfather said, stirring his coffee with a cinnamon stick.

"First batch of pancakes," Ben said, waltzing in from the kitchen. "And they're steaming hot."

He set a plate of sweet-smelling pancakes in front of her and one in front of her grandfather.

Ben poured himself a cup of black coffee and sipped it quietly. "Did you know Anna is interested in starting a women's mountaineering group?"

Anna blushed. It was simply an idea at this point, but Ben never missed an opportunity to brag about the things she put her mind to.

"That's quite an endeavor," her grandfather replied, swiping butter onto his stack. "And you're just the lady for the job."

The word *lady* made her heart sink because that was precisely the problem. She wasn't sure how many women in Seattle would be willing to join such company. Especially if there were others who might decide to boycott the bookstore and attempt to tell her exactly how they felt about her aspirations.

Greta returned from the kitchen with the rest of the pancakes and scrambled eggs. "Now, let's talk about this wedding."

Ben beamed. "My lovely fiancée would prefer a magically evergreen Christmas wedding. And she'd like to come riding in on Saint Nicholas's sleigh. That shouldn't be too hard to coordinate, right, Oscar?"

Anna glared at him playfully, and he reached for her hand under the table. The touch brought an exciting chill up her arm, and she shuddered.

"You know what would make it the best wedding of all?" she asked. "If you invited your parents so we could all meet them, and they could watch their only son marry the love of his life."

Ben was silent.

So she asked, "Will you tell us more about them?"

Greta tilted her head thoughtfully, clearly eager to hear more.

"Well, they have both worked at the university for a long while. They're good people, I suppose, but I haven't always seen eye to eye with them."

Anna nodded understandingly, wishing he would say more.

He chewed his mouthful of pancakes and then nodded definitively. "If it truly means that much to you, I think writing a simple letter can't hurt. It will be up to them if they decide to respond."

She clapped her hands with delight, then put a hand on his. Now, it really would be the most wonderful wedding.

"But I don't think they're the loving mother and father

figures you're imagining. Truly, we might be better off if they don't attend."

Anna frowned as he looked away. His tone included something of a warning, but her desire to meet the man and woman who had raised him overpowered the foreboding that stirred in her chest at his words.

Really, how bad could it be?

CHAPTER THREE

THE PAST

EMILY | MAY 1887

As Emily's eyes scanned the row of fabric, she noticed a tall, dark-haired gentleman in a well-tailored suit. She lifted her eyes to take him in, and he looked back at her. The gruff expression on his face melted into a serene smile as he took in the sight of her. He put his hand to his hat and gave her a friendly nod before returning his attention to some paperwork on the counter. She ran her hands over her loose bun to make sure there weren't any red curls escaping.

A thrill had washed over her to see the man's eyes light up when he'd looked at her. Did he think she was pretty? Did he fancy her a proper lady or only a girl? Sometimes she still felt like a schoolgirl who should be wearing a bonnet instead of a lady of seventeen.

"This all looks in order," the man said importantly to the store clerk. "Thank you for providing such in-depth records. It sure makes my job easier."

The clerk nodded enthusiastically.

"But of course, Charles." He leaned in closer before adding, "We quite appreciate the leniency that Mercer Bank has provided us."

Charles's face softened as he tipped his hat a final time before stepping out the front door causing the bell above to jingle.

In the silence that came after, her chest moved quickly with exhilarating breaths. That was the kind of man she wanted to marry. Kind, handsome, important. What more could she want in a husband?

The calico fabric stacked on the table in front of her felt soft against her fingers. One day, she'd marry a man like that. Someone established, respected, and so tall! She could hardly imagine what delight it would be to hold his arm and greet him with a kiss after a long day of working at the bank. She could arrange wildflowers on their kitchen table, roast a chicken for Sunday dinner, and make sure she looked her best when they went into the city for fancy evenings out.

What a life they could have together. Nothing like the one on her family farm. Her father was the chief of police, but it didn't pay much. Her mother spent her days collecting eggs, cleaning horse stalls, and feeding pigs. A banker's wife would certainly have satin dresses with lace hats and fine silk gloves.

Emily sighed and gathered the yard of calico her mother had requested. She handed the store clerk her coins, and he cut and wrapped the fabric in brown paper.

Outside, the rain fell as a misting shower. The clouds hung low overhead, casting gray misery over her mood. What could she do to get the attention of an important man? Was it simply a matter of being out in society and looking her best?

That twinkle in his eye when his gaze had met hers—

surely, she wasn't imagining it. It was as if a lamp had been lit behind his dark brown eyes. Thank goodness she'd worn her best dress to town. Her mother always said the emerald hue made her face look pretty.

As the mist soaked through the shoulders of her garment, she looked longingly at the horse-drawn carriage passing her in the street. How lovely it would be to ride inside one. Or so she imagined—it was a joy she'd never got to experience. A simple waste, her mother always said. Carriages were for those who wanted to waste their precious pennies.

It was almost supper time, and she quickened her pace. She couldn't wait to tell her mother about the handsome man she'd seen at the store. Maybe she'd have some ideas about how to get his attention.

As she neared their homestead, her stomach dropped with embarrassment. Her mother was respected enough around town, but there was a separation between the city ladies and everyone else, it seemed.

Now that she was finished with school, Emily decided it was time to make her own place in society.

CHAPTER FOUR

NOTHING TO FEAR

EMILY | OCTOBER 1890

Emily smoothed her red satin skirts as she sat at her husband's bedside. The white quilt was without blemish and perfectly ironed. She smoothed her hand over the soft cotton, then brought her gaze to meet her husband's feverish eyes. It was his second day with a terrible stomachache, so she'd sent for the doctor.

"Will you fetch me a glass of water?" he asked softly.

"Already brought you some, Charles," she said kindly, putting a hand to his damp forehead. "Can I bring you anything else? Shall I read you a story?"

"You've done plenty. You may go," he said brusquely.

She looked away, clenching her jaw. Much of their marriage had been like this, and she kept hoping he'd respond differently to her. He was the kind of man who preferred women to be seen and not heard.

"You don't want company?" she asked, careful not to

sound too eager—her pride was already hurt. It was a feeling she'd grown accustomed to, but it always stung when he asked her to leave. "I could bring you the newspaper—"

"Enough, please. I'd quite like to rest now."

She nodded and rose to her feet. "Of course. Sorry I disturbed you."

He touched her hand as she took a step away. "Thank you for everything. Please let me know when the doctor arrives."

Charles winced as he gave her hand a squeeze. It wasn't that he was an awful man. He was merely a little gruff and traditional. His own mother was a quiet woman who rarely spoke, and he'd expected his wife to be the same way.

She pushed away the feelings of frustration and worry, then nodded dutifully before leaving the room to check for the doctor's arrival.

Her own mother had been sick often when she was a child. She had weak lungs, the doctor had always said. The coughing seemed to last for the better part of the year, and sometimes she would be in bed for weeks needing costly medications.

But, part of the beauty of being married to Charles was that she could send for their own doctor to visit her mother anytime it was needed. Even if her husband didn't quite enjoy her company the way she'd imagined, Emily was still loved and taken care of, and so was her mother.

As she gently closed the large double doors behind her, she sighed, thinking of the day she'd first set eyes on her husband. It had been a surprise encounter and they hadn't even spoken to each other, but right away she'd known he was exactly the kind of man she'd always hoped to marry.

She rested on an overstuffed beige chair in the parlor and daydreamed of that first glimpse. It was only three years ago on an overcast day, and she'd been seventeen years old.

A knock at the door brought her back to the present with a jolt. Surely, that was the doctor come to check on Charles.

She welcomed the white-haired physician into the parlor. "Can I get you tea, Dr. Schumaker?"

"That would be lovely, thank you, dear," he replied, hanging his coat on the rack near the door. "What seems to be the trouble with your husband?"

"Terrible stomach pains," she replied. "He hardly ever complains of such things, and it has me a bit worried. He hasn't taken a bite of food since yesterday morning."

"You did well to call for me, Mrs. Watson," he said, graciously bowing his head. "If you'll direct me to his room, I'll examine him right away."

"Of course." She led him to the bedchamber and then hurried to the kitchen to prepare tea.

Her hands trembled while she loaded the silver tray. As she reached for the sugar cubes, she hesitated.

Better to be safe than disappoint a guest.

She added three cubes to the saucer before descending the stairs. It was a shame the doctor hadn't brought his wife along so she'd have someone to visit with. It got lonely in the house on her own.

Just as she reached the bedroom door, the doctor took his leave from the bedchamber. He looked up at her with a reassuring nod, then patted her shoulder gently.

"My dear, let's sit together and have a cup of tea."

She guided him to two chairs, set the silver tray down at a side table, and poured him a cup.

"I believe it to be his appendix, Mrs. Watson. Quite normal, in fact, and I can remove it in my office in a short procedure. He'll be back to work next week, and you'll have him eating all his supper in less than a fortnight."

She froze. A procedure?

"Is it dangerous?" she asked.

"Well, it's dangerous if it's not removed, but we've caught it in plenty of time. You've nothing to fear, Mrs. Watson."

Nothing he said comforted her. She absentmindedly took a sip of her tea while staring down at the sugar cubes. He hadn't taken any sugar cubes at all with his tea.

"I'll send word now to my partner. By the time we finish tea, he will arrive with a carriage to bring you and your husband to my office. Does that sound all right?"

She nodded numbly, gesturing toward the parlor doors.

When he returned, their tea and conversation dragged on, and the doctor continued to assure her that he knew what he was doing.

Watching her husband being carried into the carriage tugged on her heart more than she'd expected. He seemed helpless, his face as white as ash. He was her provider, and it was uncomfortable to see him in such a bad way.

She held his hand on the carriage ride to the doctor's office. The smell of astringent and cotton was making her stomach queasy.

"Please don't worry," Charles said. The perspiration on his forehead formed little beads that flowed in every direction down his face as the carriage jostled.

"Everyone keeps telling me that." She squeezed his hand and mustered her strength. Luckily, they had money to cover this expense. The procedure was just something to be endured. Soon her steady and strong husband would be on his feet and bidding her farewell as he rushed out the door to the bank for work. And one day, she would be with child, and he would be the one wringing his hands hoping she would be all right. She couldn't wait to hold a little one in her arms. They had so much to give a child—the very best of upbringings.

Emily leaned her head back against the carriage seat, trying to convince herself to be grateful for what she had, and trying not to be afraid she might lose it all.

CHAPTER FIVE

THE UNWASTED STARS

ANNA

Anna sat on the back porch of her grandfather's house with a book in her hand and a cup of coffee in her lap. The smell of cinnamon and the rich scent of coffee beans exhilarated her. It was a serene fall day with crisp edges and change in the air.

She had been reading more of *Anna Karenina*, and she had so many thoughts about the first few chapters. Why had Tolstoy written about Oblonsky's affair with such flippancy? And how could the Anna in the story have ever married a man she didn't seem to love who was so much older than she was?

The story was rich and had so many layers that she needed to take a break from it to read something more matter-of-fact, and Isabella Bird's *A Lady's Life in the Rocky Mountains* was exactly what she needed. The language was elegant, and yet there was so much about it that gave her practical advice for her own adventures. Also, it didn't hurt that the descriptions were beautiful. Her eyes lingered on a particularly lovely passage:

All was bright with that brilliancy of sky and atmosphere, that blaze of sunshine and universal glitter, which I never saw till I came to California, combined with an elasticity in the air which removed all lassitude and gives one spirit enough for anything.

She sighed and looked up toward the tall evergreen trees that surrounded the back of their property. As she began to daydream about her own upcoming ascent, Heather became visible through the foliage, her daughter tumbling after her into the high grass.

"*Wiiac,* my friend," Anna called out, setting her book and coffee down to walk toward them.

Ever since she'd met Heather in the woods a year prior, she couldn't help but feel genuine fondness for her and her daughter every time they met.

It was their tradition now: Sundays at noon they visited each other. This week was Heather's turn to make the five-mile trek from her cabin to visit Anna in town.

"*Wiiac,*" Heather replied.

She scooped up her brown-haired daughter, kissing her cheek softly.

"Pisha, you may play in the field while I chat with Anna. Why don't you pick flowers for her?"

The girl grinned and spun around, taking off toward the field directly behind the Gallagher house. A few yellow, blue, and crimson flowers weaved through the high grass, but they would soon be gone with the season.

"I made us coffee." She poured Heather a cup, knowing her friend would gladly accept. "How have you been?"

Heather cradled the cup in her hands. Her thick red shawl doubtless kept her plenty warm, but Anna could see her face relax into the comfort of the warmth in her hands.

"Michael can't stop talking about us both living in town," Heather said after taking her first long sip. "He knows how I feel about that. Most people don't want any more Duwamish living in town, and I'm happy to oblige."

Anna nodded as she caught a glimpse of Pisha picking daisies in the distance. She remembered well the disdain Heather felt for Seattle and the fact that her tribe had been pushed away to other land.

"Is Michael ready for you all to live under one roof? As a family?" Anna asked.

Heather grinned. "Yes. So that's the good part, I guess. Of course I would enjoy that, but I wish he would move out to the cabin with us instead. My grandmother certainly doesn't want to live in town. She'd never leave the forest or her garden."

"But how wonderful would it be to see each other more often?" Anna gushed. "You could spend more time with Michael, and we could plan dinners together whenever we wanted."

"That would be wonderful." Heather sighed. "I'd certainly like to see him more. That would be the main benefit of living here. But I simply don't want to live among people who don't want me around. Is that so wrong?"

Anna took a long sip of her coffee. "Of course not. I wish there was something we could do to change the minds of people who already have their minds made up."

Pisha returned with a yellow and blue bouquet, presenting it to Anna with a clumsy curtsy.

Anna threw her arms around the little girl and lifted her onto her lap. "It's lovely."

"Dinner. . . Pa," she said uncertainly.

The girl's language had been exploding over the last couple months, and Anna loved being able to communicate with her more and more in English, although she was still learning Lushootseed from Heather.

"And you will have a wonderful time having dinner with your pa, I'm sure," Anna said.

Heather smiled as she watched her daughter interact with her friend. Anna felt for her—it couldn't be easy to be in such a tough position. Wanting to keep her family together but also keep herself and her daughter safe from those who wished her ill because of her lineage.

After an afternoon of relaxing with one of her favorite friends, she bid them both farewell as they set out for Heather's husband's house in town. She would be overjoyed if her friend chose to move to town, but she feared that Heather might never agree to it.

When they were out of sight, Anna reclined in the grass. Evergreens swayed above her. Their dark branches lifted in harmony with the wind, dancing to an unknown rhythm, and then softly returned to stillness. A cool wind whistled through the grasses around her, and she breathed in easily. There was nowhere besides the mountain that brought her more peace, more wholeness, than the sanctuary of the forest.

Ten months. That's how much longer she had to wait until her second climb on Mount Rainier. There was much to be done—a wedding with the most incredible man in all the world, training her body to be ready for the ascent, and building a new life with Ben in the house he'd built for them a mile away from the spot where she lay.

Surely, the time would slip by like the wind through blades of grass, but she longed to feel that thin air in her lungs, to see the tops of trees far below her. It was an exhilaration she'd never felt before last summer, and now that she'd tasted it, the constant craving for adventure always remained with her.

"Ahh, here you are," Ben said, bending down to kiss her cheek.

He sat beside her, and Anna took the liberty of resting her head in his lap since no one would see them through the tall grass.

He stroked her hair gently, taking each errant strand off her face. Her skin tingled where he touched her. She looked up at his brown eyes with such love in her heart that she knew he could see it.

"I've written to my parents. An invitation to come and visit for the wedding," he said. "Although I'm afraid you imagine them to be people they aren't."

"I'll happily accept them however they are."

"The last time I saw them, I was sneaking away and ruining the extravagant university graduation party they were throwing for me." He plucked a light blue forget-me-not bloom and tucked it behind her ear. Leaning close, he whispered, "It matches your eyes."

Then he kissed her softly. The delight of the unexpected kiss sent shivers down her spine and nearly took her breath away. He pulled away after a few seconds, jumping to his feet and brushing the grass off his pants.

"Can't go too far down that road, my love," he said, voice low.

He offered his hand, and she put hers in his as she lifted herself up to stand.

"Is that the only reason you've been hesitant to see them again?" she asked. "Because you think they'll be mad you left before the party?"

"No," Ben said with a sigh. "That's easy enough to forgive, I suppose. But my father is quite opinionated. He's traditional and prefers everything in its place. Neither of my parents ever wanted me around when I was young, and I never understood why. I still don't."

She nodded. Her fading memories of her own father were warm and full of love and times spent together. She couldn't even imagine how hurtful it would be to have a father who never wanted to be with her.

"I hope they respond kindly and that you can start a new friendship with them now that you're all adults."

Ben reached for her hand and kissed it. "I hope for that too."

As they walked to the house, she remembered they were expecting a special guest for dinner.

"Levi's girl is coming tonight," she said, feeling to see if the flower was still behind her ear. It was.

"I look forward to meeting this fabled girl my best friend has said so much about," Ben replied. "I'm sure you must be excited to meet the girl he's been writing to all this time, aren't you?"

"I'm quite looking forward to it."

They arrived at the house at the moment Levi was introducing a young lady to Anna's grandfather and Greta.

"It's a pleasure to meet you both," the girl said, offering a shy curtsy. "I'm Elizabeth Grayson."

Anna surveyed the thin girl as they walked into the room unnoticed. Her hair was a golden yellow, pulled into a long braid that hung down her back. She was pretty, for certain, but there was something painfully shy about her, which made Anna cringe as the girl fumbled with how to situate her hands.

"I'm delighted to meet you," Anna said, rushing up to her.

"We've heard so much about you, Elizabeth."

The girl's green eyes widened as she took her in. "Oh my. You must be Miss Anna. You sure are beautiful."

Anna blushed. "You can call me Anna. And that's awfully kind of you to say—thank you."

Elizabeth turned her eyes down to her feet, and Levi put an arm around her shoulders.

"I'm glad you've returned to town, my dear. My family was beginning to think you didn't exist after all," he said with a satisfied grin.

"Nonsense." Greta put her hands on her hips. She looked to Elizabeth and asked softly, "How was your visit with your aunt, dear? I'm sure she was mighty glad to have you."

"Oh, she was, and it was a lovely visit. Thank you for asking, Mrs. Gallagher."

"Again, call me Greta." The older woman smiled broadly and gestured toward the dining room table. "Let's all sit for dinner, shall we?"

Ben sat himself next to Anna and put his arm around her chair, offering her the sweetest smile. It would be the pinnacle of pleasure to be married to him. His strong jaw and tightly shorn beard made him look exactly like the hunter and fisherman he was. His dark eyes held the kindest light she'd ever seen in a person. He was truly handsome, but most importantly, he treated her like an equal, something she'd dreamed of but never thought she'd find.

"How long has your family lived in Seattle, Elizabeth?" her grandfather asked as he cut the ham into thick, steaming slices.

"I've lived here all seventeen years of my life, sir," she replied, still looking at her hands.

After she spoke, a silence fell over the table, and Anna realized the girl wasn't going to say anything more.

"What does your father do?" she asked, hoping to put her at ease.

"He owns Grayson's Grocer on Front Street," she said, this time looking up into Anna's eyes.

Greta buttered her bread, smiling at the girl. "That's nice. Do you ever help him at the store?"

The pink returned to Elizabeth's cheeks again. "No, ma'am. My pa thinks it best I stay home to help around the house. I have three little sisters and a baby brother, so Ma needs all the help she can get."

Levi put a soft hand on her arm. "And it's a noble thing you do. Helping your mother, and even your aunt, over these past months. Why don't you tell them about your violin?"

Elizabeth shrugged uncomfortably, clearly ready for the attention to be shifted away from her. "I do play the violin as well."

Anna squirmed with the awkwardness. The girl was the shyest creature she'd ever encountered. She'd met squirrels with more self-confidence. It seemed the polite thing would be to invite Elizabeth to bring her violin over and play for them someday, but she could only imagine how uncomfortable the poor girl would be with them all staring at her while she performed a concerto.

Elizabeth folded her hands in her lap, glancing around the room at each of their faces. "It's an honor to be invited over for dinner."

"And a good time to announce that I've asked Elizabeth's father for permission to court her. You'll be seeing more of this pretty lady in the coming months."

For the first time, Elizabeth's face lit up. Her smile made her look like a child, and Anna couldn't help but take a liking to her. This was likely her very first love.

"I was hoping that was the case," Greta said, grinning. "You'll have to help us with the planning for Anna and Ben's wedding, dear. We can use all the womanly input we can get. If it were up to these fellas, we'd have a plain old ceremony next weekend."

The rest of the meal went smoothly while the Gallaghers chatted, leaving Elizabeth to chime in only when she liked, which proved precious little.

For dessert, Greta served a pumpkin pie made from the first pumpkin of their garden. Anna had many fond memories of making them with her in the autumn when she was younger —stewing the pumpkin, then making it into a custard with milk and eggs. The rich taste of cinnamon, ginger, cloves, and nutmeg gave her the delightful sensation of a childhood holiday.

"I spoke with Adelaide yesterday about the Ladies Library Association," she said before taking a bite of the delicious-smelling pie.

"Excellent," her grandfather said. "Our association has had the best of intentions, but I'm afraid it needs a kick in the trousers. I'm glad those ladies are finally making things happen. How are their fundraising efforts coming along?"

"There's an all-night ball planned for later this month, and a boat will sail all the way north to Victoria for the enjoyment of those donating," she replied, wiping her fingers on the crisp napkin in her lap.

Ben put an arm behind her chair. "I heard that old Mr. Yesler himself donated a large portion in honor of Sarah."

"It's such a shame that he lost her," Greta said as she began to gather dessert plates. "I wonder if he'll remarry. How old is he now?"

"Not sure," Ben replied. "I think around eighty years old."

"Oh my," Greta said, putting a hand to her chest.

Levi leaned back in his seat, putting his arm around Elizabeth's chair in the same manner Ben had. "He still visits the mill a few times a week. I'm afraid he works way too hard for being such an old man."

"Wasn't he mayor a few years back?" Elizabeth asked, her cheeks turning pink when everyone turned to look at her.

"Quite right, he was. I think it was 1885," her grandfather replied. "And how old were you then, young lady?"

Elizabeth blushed even more. "I guess I was twelve then. I remember learning about him in school."

"I did too," Anna added to try to help the girl's embarrassment. "And I remember walking by the Yesler mansion they were constructing for so many years when I was going to school."

"I quite liked when he was mayor," Greta said, her arms full with the stack of plates she'd collected. "He opposed the violent eviction of the Chinese."

Remembering the precarious situation, Anna shuddered.

After they'd said their good-byes, Levi helped Elizabeth put her thickly knit black shawl over her shoulders.

Anna grabbed both the girl's hands. "It was truly wonderful to meet you. Do come over again soon, won't you?"

"The pleasure was all mine. I can't wait to come back. Thank you for welcoming me kindly." She ducked her head and then glanced up at Levi with a small, childish smile.

Low voices behind her made Anna swing around to see her grandfather and Ben still at the table speaking in whispers.

"Wouldn't you gentleman like to say good-bye to our guest?" she asked, lifting her voice slightly.

"Yes, of course. Pleasure to meet you, Elizabeth," her grandfather boomed. He stood and strode over to her, patting her back with a rough hand. "A lovely girl for my Levi. I couldn't be happier."

Ben was beside Anna in a moment, hand extended to their guest. "A pleasure indeed, Elizabeth. Hope to see you again soon."

As Levi led Elizabeth out the front door, Anna turned to Ben. "What were you secretly discussing over there?"

Ben's face went still—he was hiding something. She looked to her grandfather, who winced as he attempted to scratch behind his back and peered toward the window.

"Please," she said. "What, pray tell, is a topic you must keep from me?"

Her grandfather sighed deeply. "Didn't want to worry you, lassie. Something happened at the bookstore this morning."

Her stomach dropped. Hopefully, it had nothing to do with her this time.

"What happened?" she asked softly.

Ben put an arm around her waist. "An older woman made a little scene at the bookstore. She had read the article and decided it was her duty to come and chastise your grandfather."

The fact that it was a woman made her feel sick to her stomach. She grabbed her light blue shawl from a hook by the door.

"Don't be upset," her grandfather pleaded. "It's nothing."

"I need a moment in the evening air. I'll be right back."

She closed the door softly and walked behind the house near the flower field that Pisha had frolicked in a few short hours earlier.

What joy that little girl had. At nearly two years old, she had no concept of the people of Seattle looking down on her for being half Duwamish. And no idea that the fact she was a woman would confine her to certain expectations for the rest of her life.

It wasn't the world she wanted Pisha growing up in, or her own child, for that matter, if she was lucky enough to have children of her own.

As she reached the trees, she looked up at the sky through the branches and thought of a poem she'd read the day before by Elizabeth Barrett Browning.

Meek leaves drop yearly from the forest-trees,
To show, above, the unwasted stars
that pass in their old glory.

A frog croaked a few feet away in the grass, which drew her attention to the ferns on the ground. Then she looked up again at the tops of the trees that had appropriately thinned for the fall and gazed at those twinkling, unwasted stars. The night air was colder than she'd expected, and it reminded her of the night she'd spent sleeping on ice the day before her injury, the day her team had gone on to summit without her.

Now that her family accepted her for who she was, it was easier to seem unbothered by the thoughts and opinions of others when it came to propriety. But in the quietness of the evening, she started to wonder what her true motivation was. Did she merely want to ruffle feathers, or did she really love climbing that mountain and being adventurous?

If she was going to be truly honest with herself, it was both. But she wasn't doing it simply to cause a stir.

Her resolve hardened like mountain ice, and her heart leapt with the excitement of climbing her mountain again.

Even if it did make prudish old ladies uncomfortable.

CHAPTER SIX

A SIMPLE PROCEDURE

EMILY

Emily's nerves were as frayed as burnt rope as her husband was whisked into another room for his procedure. It was simple, they kept saying. She exhaled through tight lips.

The doctor said it was best to remain outside the room so she wouldn't faint at the sight of blood. Probably not a bad idea. Even the metallic smell of blood made her a bit queasy. As she sat on a plush chair outside the room, she twisted a loose red curl over and over while she ruminated on the ordeal.

Her mother had needed a few small procedures as well. Nothing too concerning, only little things throughout the years. There was no one with a more positive spirit than her mother, and no one who was as sick as often.

But Charles was rarely sick. He was quite a healthy man. Whatever had caused trouble with his appendix was a mystery to her, and she hoped it didn't mean there would be more problems to come. They simply said it must be removed, and based on her husband's current condition, she believed them.

As promised, the procedure was finished before long.

Dr. Schumaker shut the door behind him and then turned to her with a kind smile. "The ether will wear off soon, my dear. It's the very newest way to provide a pain-free procedure, and we're happy to offer the service."

For a high price, no doubt, but she was grateful nonetheless. "May I go and see him now?"

"Of course," he replied, already walking down the hallway toward his office. "Fetch me if you need anything."

She pushed the door open, and the smell of blood and alcohol tinged the air. It would be the proper thing to do, to sit by his bedside as a lady ought to. He'd be happy to see her when he woke—as long as she didn't speak too much.

A rigid wood chair stood near the bedside, so she settled in, remembering the real reason she'd married Charles—to be part of society and have the means to care for her mother.

Her mother had married for love, and although she still loved Emily's father, they'd had a difficult time making ends meet as far back as she could remember. It would have been different if her mother wasn't frequently sick. Her father made a respectable income as the police chief, but they'd been constantly in debt to pay for doctors.

By the time Emily had turned fourteen, she'd decided that wasn't the life for her. If she could find herself with a man of means, it would free her family and even open up better treatment options for her mother. That was the main reason she'd never entertained the boyish advances of her childhood best friend, Levi Gallagher.

They'd been quite close. Perhaps she'd loved him once, but it hadn't been meant to be.

And now, here she was with custom-made dresses and small luxuries to brighten her days, even if it wasn't the love of a lifetime.

Her marriage wasn't romantic or overly loving, but Charles held her in high regard and was proud of her stylish and proper manner. He treated her like a queen at dinner parties, even if he rarely spoke to her at home. When she had children someday soon, there would be plenty of chatter around the house and she'd truly come into her own.

She reached for his hand and held it in her lap. It was chilly in the room, and his fingers seemed cold, so she rubbed them between her palms gently and then kissed the top of his hand.

"Wake up, my dear, and they can take us home." She leaned back in her chair, realizing how exhausted she was from the events of the day.

A few moments went by, and Charles slept on. An unsettled feeling swept over her as she squeezed his limp hand. She rushed to the door to get help.

"Doctor, it's quite cold in here," she called from the doorway. "Perhaps if we could have another blanket for Charles. And how soon should he wake?"

"He'll be awake any moment," the doctor said gaily as he returned with a look that was almost reproof. "But yes, ma'am, I'm sure I can find—"

He stopped short, his eyes on Charles.

Emily looked from the doctor to her husband's face in alarm. "What is it? Is something wrong?"

"His lips—the color. Excuse me, Mrs. Watson." He ran from the room, shouting for his partner.

Emily's shoulders trembled, dread crept inside her chest, and she gripped her husband's hand again. She felt as if she were removed from her body in a way—nothing felt right. His lips had certainly lost some color, but her mother's lips were often pale when she was sick. Her heart pounded as the beating of footsteps sounded down the hallway. Certainly, it must be an emergency for both doctors to come running with such speed. The anticipation of their diagnosis was unbearable. She needed relief from this suspended state of unknowing.

They both returned in moments, ushering her out of the room and away from the cold hand she was holding.

"I don't understand," she said, her voice cracking. "Why can't I stay?"

Dr. Schumaker sat her down again on the plush chair outside the room. "The gas we used is called ether. Given at the appropriate dosage, which it was, I assure you, it provides a safe sleep for the patient. We've never had this happen before, but it seems Charles might have reacted differently. I'll return with more information as soon as possible."

With that, he brusquely shut the door.

Her breath was coming in uneven gasps and pauses. It seemed the easiest thing in the world—to breathe—but she couldn't seem to manage it without intent focus. Her chest tightened as she thought of the worst thing that could happen. It couldn't be. And then she realized she hadn't taken a single breath since the last deliberate one.

There was clanging and commotion behind the closed door, which made her heart race even more. Surely, they could fix this. They were the best doctors in the city. If anything could be done for Charles, they would spare no expense.

Time dragged on through infinite loops of breath. Outside

the far window, a tree limb sagged with the weight of a hawk or a squirrel, she couldn't tell which. Or maybe it was only the wind. Had it started raining? She couldn't even remember what the weather had been when they'd arrived hours ago.

Just as she stood, footsteps echoed inside the room. The hinges creaked as the door slowly opened, and Dr. Schumaker drifted out, face ashen.

"I'm afraid. . . I'm very sorry, but. . ."

He cleared his throat loudly—too loud—and in that moment Emily felt the loss of her husband as if a stone were crushing her into dust.

THE DAYS after were a muted blue of air and difficult breathing.

Dr. Schumaker was beside himself and came calling to check on Emily every day. He kept babbling about appropriate dosages and recommended procedures. But the cold truth was that her husband had been buried in a deep grave with a beautiful marble stone placed at the head.

Their love hadn't been the stuff of fairy tales, but it had been solid and true. They belonged to each other, and Charles had promised to take care of her always. But now his lawyer was coming any moment to go over the affairs of the household.

An impatient knock sounded at the door, but she stayed in her chair, tea in hand. The looming grandfather clock ticked back and forth, never-ending, mesmerizing. What did it matter if the hurried lawyer had to stand for a moment longer in the November rain?

Slowly, she made herself stand. An odd sensation of

dreaming came over her as she opened the door, but there was no hope of this reality being only a nightmare.

"Mrs. Watson," the man said as he removed his hat and walked brusquely into the parlor. "I do hope I'm not disturbing you."

She gestured toward the sitting room. Her tea was already cold, so there was no point offering any to the lawyer. It was the type of thing that would have horrified her a week ago—not providing a guest with a kind word and hot tea—but the world was different now, and she with it.

"I'm afraid I do not have good news for you, so I'll get right to the point."

She nodded silently and took a seat opposite the lawyer.

"This is quite unfortunate, and I feel for you. I truly do. But your husband was in some debt at the time of his—" He cleared his throat and shook his head as if his words were in poor taste. "As a banker, Mr. Watson was intimately familiar with the loan process, and it seems he had taken out a heap of money to purchase this home and to live the life you've become accustomed to."

"What are you telling me?" The part of her that had been annoyed with him droning on vanished at once. The beat of her heart sped up as a nervous heat crept up her chest.

"You have nothing, Mrs. Watson," he said quietly. "In fact, your husband owes the Mercer Bank a significant sum of money. We're going to have to sell this house and everything in it. Then the rest of the debt falls to you."

"That doesn't make a bit of sense," she replied, taking a sip of her cold tea. Some deep part of her was afraid she'd gone completely mad. It was hard to comprehend the meaning of this man's words. Nothing was making sense anymore.

"Charles had been living in this house for quite some time before we married. And I still live here, so. . ."

The lawyer wiped his mouth with a hand and leaned toward her, his elbows on his knees. "I wish I had better news for you, I truly do. I also wish this rarely happened, but I can tell you for sure and certain that you're not the only woman who has gone from proper lady to poor widow overnight."

Widow.

No one had called her that yet. Not to her face, anyway. It wasn't necessarily a curse or an insult, but it was such a heavy word. Her mind was thick with uncertain thoughts, and wading through them proved too tiresome. She swallowed hard. She *must* sort through these thoughts, and she *must* figure out what to make of the lawyer's news.

"What do you recommend, sir?" she asked as politely as she could. "Can the loan be transferred to me?"

"I'm afraid it doesn't work that way."

His pained eyes said he was sorry, but an angry black heat burned inside her.

"What, then?" she asked, her voice rising. "Shall I join a circus or a traveling theater? What would you have me do?"

He stood, holding his hands in front of him as if in defense. "Most young ladies in your position move back in under their father's roof, ma'am. You can take a few dresses and personal items, but I'm afraid the furniture and anything of high value must be turned over to the bank."

"You keep saying that. *I'm afraid.* But I'm the one who should be afraid, shouldn't I?" She paused to collect herself. "I'm sorry, I feel. . .not myself."

He sighed and wiped a layer of perspiration from his forehead.

She cleared her throat and looked up at him. "And what of his debt? Do I owe that too?"

"In a way, you are fortunate that after your house and things are sold, you may only owe about a hundred dollars, give or take, depending on how the auction goes. Others aren't as lucky. They owe impossible sums—amounts they could never earn with a respectable job in a lifetime—and they end up working in a brothel."

Emily sucked in a breath and held it. It was as if he'd torn her clothes off and then slapped her across the face. Shame rushed in with a speed that surprised her.

"You must leave now." She stood slowly, her chin rising even though it trembled.

She needed to get this man out of her sight immediately, even if it meant being rude or brusque. The look on his face told her he was glad to be going.

CHAPTER SEVEN
TAKEN

EMILY | NOVEMBER 1890

The golden glow of the sunrise filled her room as Emily buttoned her wool dress, despising the coarseness of the fabric. She had sold most of her valuable clothing to go toward Charles's debt, but she'd purchased cheap fabric for day dresses and a pair of boots she could do farm chores in with some of the cash.

Her parents and younger sister had received her home with deep love and compassion, but she had begun to feel less and less of anything at all. There was sadness about losing Charles, but mostly she drifted through each day on the farm with little in the way of feelings.

She had grieved over Charles and still felt his absence like a missing limb. But as November dragged on, she came to realize she must pull herself out of her gloom if she ever hoped to earn the remainder of his debt, which ended up being eighty-five dollars after the furniture and artwork from the house had been auctioned.

Emily decided that after her morning farm chores, she would head into town with as much confidence as she could muster and figure out where she might get a respectable job. The audacity of that lawyer to even mention a brothel made heat rise in her chest. And to think how much she had once looked down on her childhood friend June on account of joining a brothel. She let out an exhausted breath and fastened the gold chain that held her wedding ring around her neck. Then she slipped it under her dress.

A chilling east wind blew across the low land of the farm, making the horses stomp their feet in protest. They were lovely creatures, but she would much rather ride in a fancy carriage driven by them than scoop up their droppings with a shovel. The wind brought with it the smell of many kinds of manure in various stages of decomposition. Life and death, food and waste, were all part of a continuous primordial cycle on a farm. There was a beauty to it on occasion, but right now it felt like death was coming for her next.

Tears pricked her eyes, a sensation she hadn't experienced in weeks. It was a feeling, anyhow, and she welcomed the emotion even though it burned her eyes. Her highest hope as a girl had been to marry a man of means and escape the farm. She'd wanted to be able to take care of her mother, but she hadn't even been able to care for her husband. Why hadn't she noticed the color of his lips? If she had fetched the doctor sooner, might he have lived?

Her tears flowed freely as she reached the chicken coop to collect eggs. It was a cleansing kind of sorrow, not heaving or sputtering, but large tears rolled down her cheeks as she palmed each warm brown egg.

What if she had married for love? Would she be any worse off? At least then, if she were a widow of a man she had passionately loved, she'd have the memory of a great love. Now she was left with the remembrance of silent nights, fancy meals, clothes from Paris, and Charles asking her to please stop pestering him with so many questions.

She'd never even imagined the possibility of being where she was now—a widow in debt. She was still young, but she'd already been with a man. She had belonged to someone else, and she couldn't imagine that made her very attractive to the eligible bachelors in town. And worse, she owed a debt to one of the biggest banks in Seattle. Working a lowly job in town would knock her even lower down the social ladder.

In the bright blue sky above, the sun was shining. It was not the best type of weather for wallowing, but she tried her best. When she was younger, blue skies and mild, dry weather had made her perfectly happy, but she was having an existential crisis that did not lend well to birds chirping and chickens hopping happily around her.

After she had milked the cow, she returned to the kitchen where her mother was already starting the daily bread, and her younger sister Lauren was peeling potatoes.

"It's been fun having you home again, Em," Lauren said, a grin on her face.

The girl had light brown hair in thick braids down her back. They were nearly seven years apart in age, which had somewhat stunted their sibling bond, but now that Emily was back home, it was a chance to get to know her better.

Her mother looked up from the bread she was kneading. "I know it's terrible circumstances, but it has been such a joy to have you near again."

Emily poured the pail of milk into the milk pan so the

49

cream could easily rise to the top to be skimmed off later. It was comforting to have the company of her mother and sister during the day again. Loneliness had often consumed her while Charles had been at work, unless she was lucky enough to have a guest or an invitation to visit another lady.

Her father joined them in the kitchen, dressed and ready for his day as the local police chief. "Good morning, Linda."

He kissed his wife on the cheek before sitting at the wooden table near the stove. "Shouldn't you start getting ready for school, Lauren?"

"Yes, Pa," she said, wiping her hands on her apron and then taking it off.

Her father nodded and looked to Emily. "I heard of a wealthy family who's lookin' for another cook in their kitchen. You've always made a mighty fine meal, haven't you? Maybe that's a job you could take. If you're still lookin', that is."

Emily took a deep breath and sat down across from him. The idea of working as hired help in the house of someone she might have been a guest of with Charles made her stomach turn sour.

"I'm not that good of a cook," she said with a weak smile.

She needed a job with less humiliation involved. As it was, she was barely ready to leave the house and face people in town.

Anna had mentioned that perhaps she could come work with her at the Gallagher bookstore, but hiring another person would be more than they could afford. She didn't want to be the cause of the Gallaghers losing money.

"You're welcome to stay here as long as you need," her mother said, covering the dough with a tea towel. "We absolutely love having you."

"Yes, of course," her father echoed, eyebrows raised slightly. "I thought you were lookin' for a job is all. 'Course you can stay with us forever if it suits you."

Emily let out a groan. "Thanks, Father. I know you mean well. And I do need a job. It's probably high time I find one."

"Mr. Grayson's grocery clerk is gettin' married next week. I'll have a word with him to see if the position has already been filled."

"That sounds like a fine idea. Thank you," she replied.

Her father grinned with satisfaction.

Being a grocery clerk wouldn't be so bad. Most of the wealthier people in Seattle society had maids to do their shopping, and the people who did their own shopping weren't much worse off than she was now. At least, she wouldn't have to be a maid or a cook in the home of someone she knew. That was a small mercy.

❦

Two weeks later, Emily found herself behind the counter of Grayson's Grocer wearing a white apron. She weighed beans and flour, sold eggs and milk, and greeted the customers with as much cheer as she could manage.

Most of the people who made their way through the shop were in no hurry and treated her with respect. The first few days had been long, with much to learn, but she got the hang of things before long. Soon she didn't mind her days filled with conversation and the company of strangers.

One cold morning at the end of November, Levi walked through the front door of the shop, and her heart fluttered. She recalled the last time she'd seen him. An encounter when

Anna, Ben, and Levi had stopped by her house the previous year. She couldn't remember what she had looked like exactly. Surely, she'd been wearing a silk dress and sweet-smelling powder, and her hair had been arranged in a magnificently coiled bun on top of her head.

The way he had looked at her that day, she had known he loved her still. But she had been exactly where she wanted to be, even if her heart had longed for their old friendship. And now she was too embarrassed to even say hello. How far she had fallen.

She slipped into the back room to rummage through a large barrel of apples, then she began busily stacking them again.

Mr. Grayson called her name from his office. "Emily, I think I heard the front door. Can you see if a customer is waiting?"

She shuddered at the thought of seeing Levi this way, but there was nothing to be done about it. As she rounded the corner to re-enter the shop, their eyes met.

"Oh my goodness," Levi said, taking his hat off. His eyes were wide.

"I work here." She walked to the counter in front of where he browsed the seasonings.

"I've been meaning to check in on you." His eyes were piercing with concern. "I know Anna has visited, but—"

"It's fine, of course. I didn't expect you to," she said, folding her thin arms around her chest.

"Well, I hope you've been taking good care of yourself. I heard about the matter of your husband's debt. I'm so sorry—"

Mr. Grayson breezed in from the backroom. "I thought that was you! How are you, son?"

Levi's composure changed drastically. He held out his hand to shake Mr. Grayson's, and a huge grin spread across his face. "I came by to pick up milk and flour on account of Greta asking me to. You know she makes the finest pastries this side of Lake Washington."

"Well, maybe she can teach Elizabeth how to make them too. How are things getting along with your courtship?"

A second wave of humiliation washed over Emily and she looked down, but not before Levi glanced over at her with a quick apologetic glance.

"Going well, sir," he replied. "She's joining us for dinner this evening. My family has taken quite a liking to her."

If she excused herself at that moment, it would have seemed like this news bothered her. Which it didn't necessarily, besides the fact that she'd half-expected Levi to love her forever and never marry. It was a ridiculous expectation, and she'd never even said it aloud, or perhaps even formed the thought. But learning of his courtship in this way was more than she could stomach.

Mercifully, Mr. Grayson asked her to search the backroom for a bottle of wine to give to Levi—a gift, he said. She nodded without looking back, hurrying away and through the swinging doors.

In truth, there was nothing to be upset about. Once she was back on her feet and the debt paid off, she could purchase new dresses and let the word out that she was ready to court again. It wouldn't be long before a new and wealthy gentleman moved to town and didn't mind the fact that she was a widow.

Never in her life had she felt that marrying Levi was a real option for her, but now that he was taken, something didn't quite sit right. Surely, Mr. Grayson's daughter was a fine lady, so what was the cause of her lightheadedness?

She rummaged on the shelf for the kind of wine that was asked for, and her mind went back to the days of her youth when the world was full of possibilities.

CHAPTER EIGHT
ONCE UPON A CHERRY TREE

EMILY | AUGUST 1884

Emily climbed the cherry tree to join Anna's brother in the shade. Levi had just returned from his first halibut fishing adventure, full of hope and awe for the open sea.

At just fourteen, Emily could hardly imagine traveling so far from home, but she admired her friend for being brave enough to do so. She'd missed him while he was gone.

As she sat on the branch next to him, she could feel the heat coming off his body. His nearness was intoxicating.

He exhaled slowly, and she thought she saw his lips tremble as he leaned toward her.

"Don't kiss me," she said, looking away.

"Why not?" His forehead scrunched in question. "Don't you like me?"

"I do, but not that way. You're my best friend. I've known you my whole life."

He reached for her hand. "What does that matter?"

His touch got her full attention, but she tried to ignore the butterflies in her stomach. She still saw him as a boy, not a man, even though her body told a different story. The warmth of his leg against hers reminded her how much she felt undeniably physically drawn to him. But she couldn't reconcile the idea of Levi, her friend, with these new feelings.

"Maybe you're still too young," he said, scooting away so their legs were no longer touching. "To see me the way I see you."

She shrugged. Her mind was full of sparks and confusion.

He leaned over and whispered in her ear. "Maybe one day you'll want to kiss me, and that will be the best day of my life."

CHAPTER NINE

WITH CHILD BY SUMMER

ANNA | DECEMBER 1890

T he first snow of winter came late, and Anna relished the white flakes drifting down from low-hanging gray clouds. Snow meant Christmastime, and then her wedding would be right around the corner.

The autumn had passed quickly with family dinners, getting to know Elizabeth, working at the bookstore, and planning her wedding. Elizabeth remained painfully shy but kind as could be.

There hadn't been any additional complaints from customers at the bookstore about Anna's mountaineering tendencies, but she couldn't help but wonder when they might resurface, especially as the expedition drew near. Who all knew that she would be part of a second climb? Had word already gotten around?

She squeezed her eyes shut for a moment, then opened

them to see the snowflakes out the window growing even larger.

In an exciting twist of events, Ben's parents had written a letter back to him saying they would be glad to attend the wedding. Anna couldn't wait to meet them. They were expected to arrive that very evening.

But she hadn't heard back from June, which made her heart sink. She was sure she'd sent the letter to the correct address for their new home in California, and she'd been checking for mail every day in December. Hopefully, she and her new husband, Dr. Connor Evans, were all right. Their infant son would only be about six months old, but she'd love to have them all come visit for the wedding.

It was possible the letter had gotten lost, or they simply didn't have the means to travel. Or maybe Connor's new practice was booming and he couldn't afford the time off.

Anna poured herself a cup of hot cocoa, then put two chocolate crinkles on a tea plate. She picked up her notebook that held the details for the wedding. The planning was coming along nicely. She wanted to include as many of the Irish traditions as her grandfather could recall, so that it was as similar as possible to the wedding of her own parents. Greta had made a fine silk dress of white and blue with Celtic knots sewn into the bottom hem. The Irish lace that she had ordered months ago had finally arrived. It was to go on the bodice of the dress, and also to adorn the wool bridal cloak she would wear.

In lieu of a veil, Anna planned to use whatever wildflowers they could find in the middle of December, plus a healthy dose of evergreen boughs to make a crown and bouquet. Heather had promised to scour the forest to find the best pieces the morning of the wedding, which was to be on a Sunday.

Anna moved away from the kitchen window and returned to the hearth where Greta sat happily adding the special lace to the bridal cloak. The fire crackled with warmth, and she melted into the chair beside the woman who had mostly raised her.

"Nearly finished, dear. Don't you worry," Greta said without looking up, her fingers working quickly but carefully. "That chicken roast smells divine, and the rolls should be done shortly. Are you excited to meet Ben's parents this evening?"

She sighed. "I'm delighted to meet them, and I sure hope they like me."

"Don't be silly. You're smart and lovely. They'll be honored to call you family."

She looked up to see tears glistening in the woman's eyes. "What's wrong, Greta?"

"I think it's time." She stood abruptly, placing the cloak gently on her chair. "I'll get your grandfather and tell him the time is now."

"Time for what?" she called after her.

But Greta had already hurried up the stairs.

A moment later, her grandfather came down. Greta followed after with a grin on her face and her eyes still shining.

"I was going to save this for your wedding day, but Greta thinks it ought to happen this very moment," he said, pulling out a yellowed envelope. "She's usually right about these things, so here you go."

He held out the wrinkled letter, and Anna received it with curiosity.

"You see, dear," Greta said. "We don't know what it says. Perhaps it would be better for you to read it now instead of right before the ceremony."

"It's from your mother," her grandfather said, his face full of emotion.

Her stomach dropped and she turned the letter over in her hands, her heart racing. "My mother?"

She had precious little memories of her mother, and this memento was more than she'd ever imagined receiving from her so long after her untimely death.

"Why don't you take it upstairs, dear?" Greta urged. "Take your time."

Anna nodded absently and slowly climbed the stairs to her bedroom. In swirly blue ink the letter was labeled:

For my darling Anna, on her wedding day.

After closing the door, she sat down cross-legged on her bed and eased the envelope open.

Inside was a single sheet of thick yellowed paper etched with blue ink. She glanced down to the closing—her mother's name in cursive. Tears came to Anna's eyes, but a grin crept over her face as she began reading it.

Dearest Anna,

    Moments ago, I returned from being lost in the forest for three days. I want to tell you the truth, but you're far too young. So I'll write this letter that I'll give you on your wedding day. The simple truth is I wasn't lost at all. Your father and I got into an argument and I decided I needed time to be alone. I'm terribly sorry for the worry I must have caused you, but I know you can't possibly understand why I did it until you are in love yourself.

    Marriage is full of wonderful moments but also times of discord. Your father is a good man, and I love him dearly, but that doesn't mean we don't have our differences. Today, you will marry your husband, and

I want you to know that every day won't be as perfect as I know this day will be for you. But having the love of a man who truly sees you is worth it all. Your father and I are more in love than ever now, and I know we will love each other for the rest of our days. Again, I'm dreadfully sorry for any fear I might have caused you while I was gone. Before I sat down to write this, I gave you my brooch and a small photo of me so that you can always have a part of me, even when I'm away from you.

Have a blessed wedding day, my daughter, and know that even if there are hard times with your new husband, marriage is still the most wonderful thing in all the world.

Your loving mother,
Mollie Grace Gallagher
July 1874

Anna blinked back tears and set the letter down onto her white quilt. She looked over to her nightstand that held her mother's cameo brooch and then over to her dresser where she kept the photo of her.

She must have been four years old when her mother wrote those words. It made sense that she didn't want to be honest about being away, and also that her father had seemed angrier about her disappearance than worried. He must have known she wasn't lost at all, but he had still gone out each of the three days to search for her.

What could she remember of that day? She could picture the castle upon the hill of Cashel rock and the great green fields surrounding it where sheep grazed. She could smell her mother's hair when she hugged her after returning from the woods. It still carried the scent of the outdoors and campfire.

She gingerly tucked the letter back into the envelope. She'd let Greta and her grandfather read it in time, but for now the words and the message were all hers. The photo of her mother, brown and weathered, went into her pocket. And the brooch—the one she'd worn last summer on the mountain—she pinned to the top button of her crisp white shirt.

Ben and his parents would arrive any minute, so she put a little powder over the pinkness the tears had brought and then pinned the tiny wisps of hair that had escaped her high chignon. She looked down at her checked blue, gray, and black wool skirt, smoothing her shirt into her thin belt.

Her mother would have adored Ben. And for one freeing moment, it felt as if she were there with her.

When the magic of the moment dissipated, she returned downstairs. Greta looked up from her sewing with a smile, but she didn't say a word. Anna was grateful for the silence.

After a few minutes, a soft knock sounded at the door.

She jumped up at once, calm as ever and looking forward to meeting the couple she would soon call Mother and Father.

Ben stood on the porch with a woman who was surely his mother clinging to his arm. His father stood a few inches shorter than Ben, but he had the same thick brown hair and muscly arms.

"She's breathtaking!" his mother said in a whisper.

Anna could feel the blush come over her cheeks as Ben ushered them inside the front door.

"Mother, this is my bride-to-be, Miss Anna Gallagher."

The slight woman with graying hair took Anna's hand with what seemed like awe. "You're the one who insisted my son invite us, and I will be forever grateful for that kindness."

"I'm delighted to meet you, Mr. and Mrs. Chambers." She turned to glance up at the man who was hanging his hat on a hook.

"Pleasure's all mine, Miss Gallagher. And I'm Dr. Chambers, actually."

"Dr. Chambers, oh my," said Greta as she rushed into the room. "Mrs. Chambers, we are delighted to have you over for dinner. And welcome you into our home, and our family."

"Thank you kindly. And please call me Beth."

Her grandfather and Levi appeared in the front door, returned from chopping wood. They placed their logs near the fire, then heartily greeted their guests.

"Dinner will be ready in minutes," Greta said, wiping her hands on her pinstriped apron. "Why don't you all have a seat at the table?"

"I'll help you," Anna said, following her.

"No, dear. You stay and visit. Levi, will you give me a hand?"

"Yes, ma'am." Levi put his arm around Greta, and they whispered all the way to the kitchen.

"You have a lovely home, Anna," Beth said as she sat. "I adore the magnificent view you all have from the house."

Anna smiled, wondering if Ben had already told them of their plans and her prior attempt. "Thank you. I hope you're all situated in Ben's house for the visit."

"We insisted on renting an apartment for the week." Beth smoothed a napkin on her lap. "We don't want to be there for your first nights as husband and wife."

Ben blushed, a rare occasion, and Anna enjoyed the sight immensely. How odd it must be for him, though, to be with his parents again after leaving them abruptly years ago. She hoped the morning had gone well since their train had arrived from California.

"That's awfully kind of you." Glancing to Ben, she added, "Did you all have time to catch up today?"

Ben seemed to know exactly what she meant. "We spoke of the past, and I told them a little about you, but I wanted to save most of it for you to tell."

She swallowed hard, smiling over at her grandfather who winked at her. "Well, Ben and I are going to climb Mount Rainier this summer."

Beth blinked a few too many times, but her smile didn't waver. Dr. Chambers made no attempt to hide his confusion.

"I'm afraid the next thing you're going to say is that the enormous snow-capped mountain I see out the window is Mount Rainier," Beth said, her eyes wide.

"Yes, ma'am, it is," Anna replied.

"Well, won't you be with child by summer?" Beth asked, concern etched in her eyes.

Ben cleared his throat and described their plans to join the mountaineering team, leaving his mother's question unanswered. His father was solemn and hadn't opened his mouth since sitting at the table.

It wasn't that Anna hadn't thought about the possibility of getting pregnant within the year, but she hadn't yet considered it happening so fast as to ruin her chance to climb the mountain again. She didn't know anything about how mountain climbing might affect a pregnancy, but the simple risks of falling, slippery ice, and rocky descents suddenly seemed incompatible with a vulnerable baby inside her.

Greta and Levi returned with platters of steaming food— roasted chicken, corn on the cob, and roasted parsnips.

"And we have an apple crumble for dessert," Greta added before sitting down.

Anna shifted in her seat and glanced at Ben, who seemed to feel her sudden discomfort. Why hadn't they sat next to each other? She longed to hold his hand under the table and have the opportunity to whisper things to him alone.

Dr. Chambers finally spoke up. "This looks delicious, Mrs. Gallagher. Thank you kindly for your hospitality."

Anna studied his face, looking for some sign of his thoughts about the climb or her being with child by summer, but he seemed more interested in the roasted chicken.

"Anna, I'm sure it will all work out," Beth said. "I certainly approve of a woman setting an example for others to follow."

That was a welcome sentiment, and she blew out a relieved breath.

"Did you already attend university?" Beth asked, putting a pat of butter on her mashed parsnips.

Anna's heart sank again. "No. I did graduate from high school a few years back."

"Excellent," Dr. Chambers said. "I've heard good things about the Washington Board of Education. How old were you when you graduated? And what sorts of subjects did you study in your final year?"

"I was sixteen," she replied. "I believe the last year we were taught history, geometry, astronomy, botany, and one more subject that I forget."

"The Constitution," Greta announced. "I remember learning along with you on that subject."

"Yes, that's right," she said, relieved.

"Anna seemed to enjoy the year prior to that. They did more English analysis, philosophy, that kind of thing," her grandfather added.

She nodded with a smile at him. "Since then, I've been working at our family bookstore."

"A bookstore. How wonderful." Ben's mother took a small bite and then looked at Greta, offering an appreciative nod.

"This is certainly delicious. Did you grow these parsnips yourself?"

"We sure did. Anna and I have quite the garden during the growing season. We can show you the root cellar after dinner, if you like." Greta reached for her husband's hand, clearly having a great time.

Anna shifted again in her seat, uncomfortable as she'd ever been at her own dining room table. Ben's parents were city people, both with university educations. They did not climb mountains or have root cellars. But they were kind, and she was grateful they seemed to accept her.

After the meal, she and Greta took Beth out to see the root cellar. They bundled up with coats and hats and crunched through the light snow covering.

Beth marveled at the way the cellar sloped underground and at how many vegetables and preserves they had inside.

"It's a right plentiful stock," she said warmly.

As they returned to the house, Beth linked her arm with Anna's. "There are certainly ways to avoid pregnancy. I can give you some ideas."

Anna nodded, stunned at the candor. "Oh. Thank you."

She realized, as everyone put shoes and hats on, that the evening was over and she wouldn't have any time alone with Ben. His parents said their farewells, and he kissed her cheek before they began walking back to town to catch the street trolley to the hotel.

As she watched them walk away, she leaned against the wooden side of the patio beam. The snow-dusted earth rested gently while her nerves lit with confusion.

Slowly, one of the distant figures turned, picked something up from the frozen ground, and then headed back toward the house. Relieved, she walked down the steps to meet Ben. But as the figure grew closer, she realized it was his father.

Dr. Chambers held out a flower—a buttercup winter hazel, graceful on its stem and pale yellow. "For you, Anna. It was lovely to meet you."

She smiled graciously and took the dark green stem from his fingers. "Thank you, Dr. Chambers. It's an honor to have you here for the wedding."

He smiled down at her with an unreadable expression. "I sure hope you'll remember your place though. You know what I mean."

"Do I?" she asked, tilting her head in question.

"No need to play coy with me, Miss Gallagher. Just because my son doesn't admit to being embarrassed that his woman is climbing mountains, it doesn't mean he isn't. He was raised better than that."

He tipped his hat with a smirk, then hurried back down the icy road.

A cold sweat covered her chest and neck, while a warm anger filled her insides. A type of shame she'd never felt before came over her in a way that nearly caused her to heave.

He was wrong about Ben.

Wasn't he?

CHAPTER TEN

YOU MUSTN'T WASTE YOUR LIFE

EMILY | JUNE 1886

Emily had just graduated from school at sixteen, and Greta had thrown a proper tea party to celebrate with Anna and June. After the cakes and cookies had been eaten, Emily donned her straw hat lined with lace and a single ostrich feather, kissed her friends, thanked Greta profusely, and walked out the door feeling like the luckiest girl in the world.

The sound of footsteps behind her made her turn on her heels.

"May I walk you back to town?" Levi asked from the porch.

Her heart fluttered. He stood with both hands in his pockets, cheeks flushing, but his green eyes were set with determination. His light brown hair fell in soft waves around his ears.

"Of course," she said, noticing how tall he'd become as they fell into an easy stride with each other, as they always had.

He offered his arm. "Congratulations on being done with your schooling."

"Well, I would have preferred a finishing school, you know, but state-mandated education shall do just fine. That's what Mother says anyway."

The feel of his arm was comforting and exhilarating all at once. They had been friends since she'd played with Anna after school when she was about six years old. Levi had been hesitant to join in with them, being a couple years older, but soon they were all close, along with June.

Levi swallowed hard, not taking his eyes off her. "I hope we'll still get to see you around here."

His eyes were saying a good deal more, but she ignored the gaze, not wanting to confront that quite yet. Or possibly ever.

"I plan to call on Anna as often as I can. And I hope to attend many parties in town this summer."

"You hope to catch the eye of an eligible gentleman."

It wasn't a question.

"Of course I am!" She released his arm, suddenly self-conscious at the touch.

He stopped abruptly, turning to face her. "Let me court you. I know you better than anyone. I can make you happy, Em."

He put both of his hands gently on her shoulders.

The touch made her shudder. She'd imagined kissing him many times. He was the only boy she knew that put a confusing thrill in her body.

Her voice went quiet. "And what about my mother? It's not only about things I want to buy. It's about being part of society and having the means to have the best doctors for my mother."

"I promise if we marry that we'll live in the city, and I'll have money—"

"Don't say that," she said, heat rising to her chest. "You can't promise those things."

"You're the most beautiful woman I've ever seen."

His eyes searched hers, but she glanced away.

"Levi." She paused and then started walking again, quickly this time. "Don't you want the best for me? And I also have to think of my mother."

He hurried to catch up with her. "More than anything, but I would dedicate my life to creating a name for myself, a place in society for us, for you. I would do it gladly to make you happy."

"That's exactly what I'm afraid of!" She nearly shouted it, but cleared her throat and gathered herself like the lady she was. "You mustn't waste your life trying to make *my* dreams come true. It's nonsense. You should do what you want, and I'll do what I want. We can always remain friends."

"No." His eyes narrowed. "I want you, Em. It's all I want in life. You in the morning, you when I fall asleep. I want to work hard to give you the life you deserve."

Her breath came faster, and she folded her arms as she walked. It was possible he could provide the life she hoped for. It happened, but it was rare—rising up into society. She wanted to believe it was possible, but the lump in her throat told her it wasn't the right thing to do. Letting him slave his life away to give her an easy one. Even the thought made her feel terrible about herself.

If she married a kind gentleman who was already wealthy, it would be no trouble. The man wouldn't need to change anything about himself.

If she let Levi court her, she would let herself finally love him the way he loved her, and they would marry and have children soon after. How could he possibly change their station with mouths to feed?

"I can't. I'm sorry, Levi. Forgive me if I let you believe otherwise."

She picked up her skirts and ran down the street toward home.

CHAPTER ELEVEN

THE POLICE

EMILY | DECEMBER 1890

Emily dressed in the finest dress she still owned—green satin with white lace at the hem and collar. She wrapped her white shawl around her shoulders and set out for the Gallagher home. Anna wouldn't be there. She'd be having lunch with Ben's parents and then touring the new business district in Seattle that had been built since the Great Fire.

Greta had invited her over, along with some of Anna's other friends, for a surprise bridal tea. They'd spend the afternoon arranging for the tea and making other wedding preparations, then they'd surprise Anna when she returned home from the evening out.

As she came to the dirt road that led to the Gallagher home, the evergreen trees seemed to grow even taller. There was a light dusting of snow on their green branches and red holly berries near the ground. It would make a lovely backdrop for their small ceremony.

A figure emerged from the woods. It must be the Duwamish friend she'd heard about. The woman reached the house before Emily, and so she spent the last few minutes of the walk praying Levi wouldn't be home.

When she knocked on the door, it was slightly ajar. Merry voices came from inside, along with a harmonica to the tune of "Joy to the World." Hesitantly, she pushed the door open, walking up to the group of women chatting at the kitchen table. Oscar sat near the fire, making the festive music.

Greta pushed away from the table to greet her. She wore a red calico dress with a sprig of holly pinned to her lapel. The stray white curls that fell out of her bun and around her face would have made her look young if it weren't for the color. "Good to see you, dear. This is Heather, a good friend of Anna's. And this is Elizabeth. Levi's been courting her."

Emily's stomach soured. She'd known it was a possibility for the girl to be there but had fervently hoped it wouldn't be so. She swallowed the lump in her throat and nodded kindly at both women.

Elizabeth smiled shyly. "Wonderful to meet you."

The young girl's hair was in two braids with silver ribbon tied in bows at the ends. Clearly, her mother wasn't quite ready to let her go.

"I've heard much about you, Emily," Heather said, rising to her feet as Greta had. "I'm deeply sorry for the loss of your husband."

Elizabeth gasped, putting her hand up to her mouth. "Such a terrible thing. I hadn't a clue about it. My condolences as well."

Emily frowned. "It's nice to meet you ladies."

Greta hurried her to a seat at the table where they were putting popcorn and bright red cranberries through twine.

"This lovely garland will be strung all over the house and the porch. It smells nice too, doesn't it? We can leave it up for the wedding. It should last until day after tomorrow."

With a nod, Emily moved toward the kitchen table, having to hold her skirts in to pass Elizabeth, who was still standing dumbly in the way. She lowered herself into a chair, busying her hands and trying to ignore Elizabeth's gaze.

Did the girl know she'd been such good friends with the man she was courting?

It made her feel terrible that she even cared. She had no claim over Levi. They had been best friends once, but that was a long time ago. She ought to be happy for him that he'd found a girl for whom he wouldn't have to work his whole life to raise up in society. Elizabeth would probably be perfectly content to live within whatever means he provided.

But why did her heart ache at the thought of Levi with someone besides her? He hadn't courted a single girl that she knew of. Not since he'd asked her and she'd tossed him away. It had been the right choice at the time. And it was still the right choice. Even if Levi wasn't taken, she still wanted to return to the kind of life she'd had with Charles.

Didn't she?

The sounds of hooves stomping and wheels creaking in the distance drew her attention to the window.

Greta stood, untying her apron and returning it to its hook. "Now who could that be?"

Emily stood to join her, and the two women went to the porch to watch the carriage travel down the dirt road to the house. She was glad for the change of scenery. And whoever it was would probably be better company than someone who made her think constantly of what she couldn't have.

"Well, I'll be. . ." Greta laughed and clapped her hands

together. "It's June and Dr. Evans. Anna will be beside herself with joy!"

Delight swelled in Emily's chest. A childhood friend— someone who knew her better than perhaps anyone else, save Anna. It would be balm to her soul to spend time with her.

When the carriage came to a stop in front of the house, Dr. Evans jumped out and took his hat off. "Good day, Mrs. Gallagher. I hope we're not disturbing you. June insisted I drop her here before I checked us into the hotel."

June emerged from the carriage in a yellow walking jacket and a full light blue skirt. It was a nice choice for traveling— tasteful and elegant, yet comfortable enough to withstand trains and carriages.

A stab of longing went through her, but she pushed it aside to welcome them.

"What a wonderful surprise," she said as she rushed toward June.

June's hazel eyes widened, and she threw her arms around Emily, squeezing her tight. "Well, if it isn't my dear friend come back to me."

Emily blushed, thinking of her former embarrassment to be associated with June. It had made sense at the time. June had been a prostitute, and she had been a lady trying to make a place for herself in society.

June must have no idea about Charles, unless Anna had written her about it. She had meant to send word to her, but after the gloom had taken over, she hadn't really done anything she'd meant to.

June reached back into the wagon, retrieving a wicker basket with a cooing baby inside. "He's getting quite heavy, especially for how small he used to be."

Dr. Evans reached to put his hands underneath the basket as June lowered herself to the ground.

"You are truly wonderful, my love." June kissed him on the cheek, making his face turn a light shade of pink.

"I'll let you ladies settle in while I take our things to the hotel." He tipped his hat and then disappeared into the carriage, tapping his hand twice on the roof.

Heather and Elizabeth came out of the front door as the carriage sped away.

"It's good to see you, June," Heather said, putting her arm around her. "How is little Joseph doing? How were your travels from California?"

"He's doing marvelous, but the train was dreadful." June's eyes turned toward Elizabeth. "And who's this young lady?"

"A pleasure to meet you, ma'am. I'm Elizabeth Grayson." She looked as if she wanted to reach out her hand but couldn't decide if she should since June's arms were full.

"Nice to meet you, Elizabeth." June looked past the group into the kitchen. "Where's Anna?"

"She's showing Ben and his folks around town," Greta said triumphantly. "I've secretly gathered these ladies to help with decorations, and then we have a surprise tea planned for Anna when she returns. What a brilliant sight it will be for her to see you here as well."

The women settled into the dining room, which Emily noticed was starting to shrink with an excess of people in its confines. Heather held baby Joseph while June got to work on the garland. Emily was forced to sit right next to Elizabeth, and she even had to scoot toward her to make room for June's chair.

"Are you a new friend of Anna's?" June asked, looking over at Elizabeth.

The girl paused a moment, waiting to see if Greta would answer for her. The older woman merely smiled, so she spoke. "Levi's courting me, ma'am."

"That's wonderful," June exclaimed, smiling broadly. "It's about time he found someone. And goodness, please call me June. I've been called worse." She winked at the girl. "So much must have changed since we left town, even though it's been but a few months."

Greta locked eyes with Emily, who frowned slightly and shook her head.

"Actually, June, you and Emily should have some cocoa on the porch chairs to catch up. I'm sure Joseph will be fine in here. And Heather might even let the rest of us hold him."

Heather laughed softly but didn't let go of the blond infant sleeping happily in her arms.

"Perfect," June said as she stood. "Shall we?"

Emily nodded and they re-settled on the porch. Greta brought them steaming mugs with chocolate crinkles on an elegant glass plate.

"You're truly radiant," Emily said, gazing with wonder at her friend. "You look happy, and your outfit is divine."

"Thank you. How's Charles? Is he still a snobby, grumpy man?" June grinned at her.

Her friend was clearly teasing, but the familiar coldness came over her, the chill that helped her hold all the grief at bay. Yet in June's presence, someone who'd seen her cry an uncountable number of times and had become a woman alongside her, Emily let the walls down. As she did, she realized much of her sadness had already subsided.

Did she truly miss Charles?

She missed the warmth of his embrace, the look in his eye when he said he loved her, and holding tightly to his arm at plays and dinners. But passion had never colored their lives, not truly. Now that the dust of grief was starting to settle, that was clearer than ever.

"Charles has passed," she said softly.

"Oh dear! What happened? Are you all right?"

Emily filled her in on the last few months.

"And would you believe our lawyer mentioned that women *like me* often end up at brothels?" She blushed deeply, ashamed and waiting for a subtle yet triumphant look in June's eyes, but she found only sympathy.

"Sounds like a fool." June smoothed her skirt and reached for a cookie. "That man doesn't know how many people you have that love you."

"I can't even say how sorry I am I ever stopped speaking with you," Emily said with tears in her eyes. "I had no idea what you were really going through. You must have felt hopeless and alone."

June put a hand on Emily's knee. "I'm quite happy with how my life has turned out. And that you and I are friends again."

Emily nodded, wiping away tears that hadn't fallen yet. "It's truly a delight to have you back. How's life in California?"

"We're settled and not a soul has any idea about my past. It's divine," June said with a twinkle in her eye. "But tell me more about you. Where are you living, and are you working somewhere to pay off Charles's debt?"

She sighed deeply. "I've ended up as a grocery clerk for Elizabeth's father, of all people."

Understanding flashed in June's eyes, and she mouthed the word "oh."

"Yes, it's quite the mixture of embarrassment and jealousy, if I'm to be perfectly honest."

"Do you still have feelings for him?" June asked, lowering her voice.

"I will always feel something for him. He was my best friend, and perhaps I loved him when we were young. But I never thought friendship was the main ingredient for a proper marriage."

June twisted her mouth into a half-smile, clearly holding her tongue.

"I do see things more clearly now, however," she went on. "And I long for that closeness I had with him. I saw him about a year ago when he stopped by with Anna and Ben. It was like a magnet was still drawing us together. I could see in his eyes that he still loved me, but what was to be done?"

"You followed your heart by marrying Charles," June said, taking a sip of tea. "You always wanted a fine house and a place in society, and that's nothing to be ashamed of."

"But look where it's brought me," she said, exasperated. "And now I miss that intimacy with Levi more than ever."

She ducked her head, realizing she wasn't whispering anymore. The women inside were busy adoring the baby and chatting. She thought of Elizabeth—young and innocent. No demands, no expectations. She probably loved Levi unconditionally.

"I'm afraid it's too late though," she said, resigning herself. "Elizabeth is a fine girl. I'm sure she'll be good to him. And I can live out my days as a spinster."

June laughed merrily despite the despondency in Emily's voice. "Just when you think all is lost, that's when you'll find your way."

Greta opened the door and joined them. "Anna will return soon. Let's get this garland hung and set up the holiday bridal tea."

Emily followed her into the kitchen, and June whisked the baby into her arms.

"Your first husband passed a long while back, didn't he, Greta?" June asked as she held one end of a cranberry and popcorn garland while still holding the baby.

Greta nodded matter-of-factly. "And in a small way, I grieve him still. I can't help that. It's simply the way of it."

"How did he die?" Emily asked, looking down at her hands as she took the other end of the garland June held.

"The doctor told us after his first stroke it was likely there'd be another. He'd already lost much of his mobility, and I spent a lot of time talking and reading with him," Greta said with a fond smile. "We would reminisce about our lives in Sweden and our journey to America—the three-and-a-half months we spent in a covered wagon on our trek to Washington Territory."

"Did you have any children together?" Elizabeth asked softly.

"We did not, dear," she replied. "And at that stage, all we could do was look back sadly at our inability to have children. That empty space we'd thought could be filled by the presence of other people's children still caused a longing inside us both. Perhaps if we'd stayed in Sweden and could have been around our nieces and nephews, and the children and grandchildren of close family friends in our town, we might have been able to satisfy that deep-rooted desire."

"I'm terribly sorry," June said. "I had no idea. Did your husband have another stroke?"

"Yes, after a few months, the doctor's words came true, and he suffered another one. Or that's what we had to assume. I found him still as a stump one morning, and I knew his spirit was gone." She shuddered at the memory. "But now I'm fifty-six years old, I had the privilege of helping to raise Levi and Anna, and I'm happily married to the sweetest Irishman who ever lived. I'm a lucky gal indeed, wouldn't you agree?"

They all nodded in unison, and Emily found hope in her words. She took the small mercy offered to her, folded it up neatly, and stored it thoughtfully in the reserves of her mind. She needed those words to be true, so she tried her best to believe them.

She hurried to put the finishing touches on the plate of holiday treats she was bringing to the festively decorated table. About an hour later, a figure emerged on the dirt drive, moving quickly. But it wasn't Anna. It was Oscar, and he came through the front door with an alarming burst.

"It's the bookstore," he said, out of breath.

"What happened?" Greta asked.

"I've been with the police for the last hour. Someone vandalized it again."

CHAPTER TWELVE

THE PROMISE

ANNA

Anna could tell something was amiss as she walked up the porch steps. There were multiple voices coming from inside, all speaking at once.

As she opened the door, she found the kitchen full of her favorite ladies.

"What are you all doing here? June!" She rushed to her friend.

"It's wonderful to see you, Anna." June shifted Joseph to her other hip as she embraced her friend. "We got in this afternoon. Sorry I didn't write back. I meant to."

"The police are looking into it now." Her grandfather's voice carried in from the dining room before he walked in.

Greta glared at him. "Oh, Anna, we were hoping to surprise you with a special tea with all your friends. But I'm afraid we have some. . .news."

"Is everyone all right?" she asked, concern etched in her brow.

"Everyone's fine, lassie. But while I was out to lunch, someone painted a ridiculous threat all over the front of the bookstore. *Know your place or someone might teach you a lesson.*"

Anna felt sick to her stomach. She remembered the words Ben's father had said to her the other night when he'd given her the winter flower. He had also come down with a terrible headache after lunch and had gone back to the hotel early, leaving her and Ben to show Beth around Seattle. She didn't even want to let her mind think it could be her soon-to-be father-in-law. Surely, he wasn't that cruel.

Perhaps it was simply the same man who had thrown the brick.

"I can't believe it," Anna said, folding her arms in front of her chest.

"Everything is fine. The police helped your grandfather cover the paint with a tarp for now, and we'll repaint as soon as the weather allows," Greta said, sighing heavily. She turned to her husband. "But for now, for the next hour, let us ladies have this time, all right?"

"Yes, ma'am," he said, turning to head back up the stairs.

"Greta has planned a delicious tea for you, Anna," June said, passing her baby off to Heather. "You must sit and let us serve you special Christmas treats. We have much to catch up on."

Anna nodded, trying to calm her nerves. She didn't want their hard work to be in vain, but she also couldn't imagine eating anything with her stomach in knots. She looked over at Emily and smiled.

"I'm glad to see you, Emily," she said as she took a seat at the table.

"I wouldn't miss it," her friend replied.

Emily's usual straight posture was slumped, and her smile didn't touch her eyes. It must be hard being in her position.

As Greta and June brought trays from the kitchen, Heather smiled at her. "It's wonderful to see you getting married, Anna. Don't let the bookstore situation get in the way of your happiness."

Of course, Heather was right, like always. "Yes, thank you. I'll try."

Heather nodded slightly as if to dismiss the topic. "I'm going to take my daughter to the reservation across the bay for an extended visit at the end of January. My grandmother is not up for travel during the winter season. She says she'd rather stay put near the fire. Would you mind paying her a visit in early February while I'm gone? Maybe stay for a meal?"

"I can definitely visit Kiyotsa," she replied. "I'd be glad to."

It would be a fun trip. She remembered how the old woman had come alive during the salmon fishing season she'd joined them for, and now Anna considered her a friend.

Heather leaned forward. "Promise?"

"Absolutely," Anna said. It was clearly important to her friend, not that she would have forgotten anyhow.

The special tea was extravagant indeed. Everything one could imagine for a Christmas tea—hot cocoa, peppermint sticks, and chocolate crinkles warm from the oven with a fine dusting of sugar.

As soon as the chatting had come to a lull, Emily stood. "If you'll excuse me, I'm awfully tired and should be heading home before dinner."

"Thank you for coming," Anna said as she joined her by

the front door. "You'll stand up with June and me at the wedding, won't you?"

Emily's eyes didn't meet hers as she wrapped her wool shawl around her. "I love you, Anna, but I don't think I'm ready for that yet."

"I understand," she replied quietly.

Emily walked down the porch steps in a hurry as the weak sunshine dipped below the December clouds.

At the end of the road, a horse-drawn carriage passed her as she walked away. Anna remained on the porch and leaned against the wood frame until it arrived. Much to her surprise, both Ben and Dr. Connor Evans stepped out.

"Hello, Anna," Connor said cheerfully as he stepped out of the carriage. "I ran into your fiancé at the hotel as he was dropping his mother off. I insisted he ride back with me to your house."

Ben looked unimpressed and offered a shrug and a thin smile. She resisted laughing out loud. He clearly did not want to join the man who had once courted her, but there must not have been a polite way to decline the offer.

"Well, I'm glad you're both here," she said. "Greta always enjoys a lot of company for dinner."

She paused. "Ben, will your parents join us as well?"

"No, my mother said she's had a full day and wants to rest in the hotel. Hopefully, my father already got some rest this afternoon."

"Yes, I hope so," she said, biting the inside of her cheek.

Connor clapped Ben on the back as they walked up the porch steps, but she saw Ben give him an irritated look, which made Connor withdraw his hand.

Once inside, June rushed up to her husband, kissed him on

the cheek, and then handed him their baby, whom he took with delight.

"Darling, I think I'll call on Lou Graham while we're in town to have a quick tea and say hello," June said.

Connor stopped short. "That certainly would not be a good idea, and I won't allow it. Imagine! Walking back into that brothel. Don't even entertain such an idea, June."

She waved the concern away with a smile. "I'll simply send her a note, and we can meet at a restaurant."

Connor stood his ground. "No."

June laughed, seemingly unconcerned with his sternness. "We'll chat later about it, my love."

Anna knew that tone. June planned to do exactly as she pleased, and the thought made her glad. Her friend hadn't changed a bit.

"You two ought to move back to Seattle at some point," she said, longing to be around June more often.

"We quite like California, don't we, June?" Connor said, his mood lifting.

"Oh, Anna, it's wonderful there. You must come and visit. The sun is always shining, everyone is sophisticated, and there's always a new play to be seen."

"Speaking of plays," Ben said. "My parents invited us to see a play with them before they leave next week. If you're interested, that is."

"Won't you be on a honeymoon?" June asked.

"We're going to stay at the new Occidental Hotel for an evening, but we're going to take a longer trip in early spring when the weather warms a little. Somewhere in the forest."

"You two were made for each other," June said, clearly amused.

Anna laughed. "Tell your parents I'd love to see a play. I've never seen one."

"Then we must," Ben said.

She kissed his cheek and stood. "I'm going to grab a bottle of wine from the cellar."

"Would you like company?" he asked.

She smiled broadly in reply.

It was a mild evening, so she only put a light shawl over her shoulders. Ben followed behind her out the door, then grabbed her hand as they neared the steps to the cellar.

She shuddered from the cold despite his warm hand and waited for her eyes to adjust to the dark before walking into the underground cellar.

"Who would do such a thing to the bookstore?" she asked. "Do you think it's the same man who threw the brick?"

"Hard to say. Let's hope so." Ben blew on some dusty wine bottles on a shelf.

"I'm worried," she said, folding her arms. "We shouldn't have told anyone about our upcoming trip this summer."

"You don't need to hide who you are." He turned from the shelves and wrapped both his arms around her waist.

The touch sent a tingle down her spine.

"Not to you. But apparently me climbing mountains makes a number of people angry. Angry enough to destroy things that matter to me." She sighed. "That's not even the only thing bothering me though. I feel badly for Emily right now. Having to go to a wedding only a few months after her husband died? Am I a bad friend for asking her to come?"

"You're overthinking things." He stroked the side of her neck with his finger, then kissed her cheek.

"Well, I know that marrying you is the right thing to do anyhow," she said, smiling up at him. "And now I've met your parents too, so I know pretty much everything about you."

Her thoughts came to rest again on Ben's father, but she told herself it was nothing. Enough worrying.

He grabbed her hand and walked backward a step until he was leaning against the dirt wall of the cellar. He put both of his hands on her cheeks and bent his head to kiss her.

As if there hadn't already been enough pent-up passion, her knees weakened as he deepened his kiss. Two more days and this man would be all hers.

But she pulled away. Something else was still heavy on her mind.

"Your father seems. . .displeased with the idea of me climbing."

He resumed his full height and tilted his head down at her. "He's an odd man, and I'm not too concerned with his minor displeasures."

"He wouldn't act on that, would he? I mean, do you think—"

"What made you think that in the first place?"

Anna sighed. "He said something to me privately the first night I met him. That I ought to remember my place."

He cringed. "That definitely sounds like something he would say. I'm sorry. Does it make you uncomfortable to be around him? I'll send them right home if that's the case."

Of course that wouldn't be necessary, but the words comforted her. She really was the most important thing to him in the whole world.

"Never mind. My thoughts keep spinning, but you're right. I'm likely overthinking."

Ben wrapped his arms around her and kissed her until she could think of nothing else.

CHAPTER THIRTEEN
SOMETHING INTIMATE

EMILY

Emily walked slowly, as if to another funeral. A wedding was a joyous occasion, and she ought to keep a smile on her face as much as possible, but it was difficult. Of course, she was delighted for Anna and the happiness she'd found, but it was hard not to dwell on her own misfortune, and even more so while Levi was attending with his soon-to-be wife.

Why did it bother her? She could have chosen him, and she hadn't. She was all he'd wanted, and she'd said she was looking for something different and that he should look elsewhere. It had been the right choice at the time. But what was the right choice now?

Not that it mattered. He was taken.

Her wool cloak felt heavy and comforting. She wrapped it tighter around her, hoping to maintain what little body warmth she had. Her frame had become thinner than ever this winter, but not for lack of meals being offered. She couldn't eat much at once without feeling queasy. It nearly brought her mother to tears, but eating like a bird was the best she could do for now. Merely enough to sustain her, enough to keep moving, to keep living. One day, her appetite would return, and she'd promised her mother to eat everything in sight. Emily truly hoped that day would come.

The Gallagher house was a sight from a picture book. Candles had been laid all around the porch that wrapped around the dwelling. The garlands of popcorn and cranberries were strung neatly, bringing a wonderful Christmas scent, and a few songbirds.

The wooden chairs from the dining table and the porch had been set up on the grass along with quilts and blankets facing the forest where a candelabra glowed a safe distance from the tree line.

"I'm glad you came," Greta said, stepping beside her. "How's your mother?"

"She's not feeling well. Otherwise, she would have come."

"Well, you can sit with me up front, if you like. And do help yourself to the eggnog. There's a large kettle of it over the fire. Oscar put in both brandy and rum. It'll warm you up." Greta winked at her and then went off to greet a carriage that was pulling up to the front of the house.

It wasn't a large crowd, perhaps thirty people, most of whom she knew. Heather and her family, June and Dr. Evans with their baby, and, of course, Elizabeth with her family. Levi was nowhere in sight, thankfully. If she could avoid seeing the two of them together, it would spare her heart the pain. Because surely, that sight would be too much. It was simply a matter of looking. And if she didn't look toward them, she wouldn't see.

I'll keep my eyes on Anna and Ben and hope that one day I'll find a love like that.

She wondered if Anna was upstairs in her room and figured it would be a good place to escape to even if the bride was elsewhere. She walked toward the house, looking forward to the warmth of the fireplace.

Inside, the house was quiet but for fire crackling in the hearth. Smells of pot roast and potatoes came from the kitchen, and a woman she didn't recognize stood at the cookstove tending to it. Probably one of Greta's friends who'd offered to mind the food so Greta could mingle.

Emily slipped up the stairs and nearly barreled straight into Levi.

"Pardon me," he said before looking up. "Oh, how are you?"

Her heart raced like a scared bird. She could flee down the stairs and refuse to speak with him. She was still a grieving widow, and odd behavior wasn't unexpected.

Did *he* see her as a grieving widow? Or perhaps he still saw her as a young woman full of life.

"I was looking for Anna," she said quietly, glancing everywhere but at his eyes. "To see if she needed anything."

"She'd love your company," he said, coming down a step toward her. They were only a foot apart now. "June is with her. It'll be good for the three of you to have a few minutes together. Like old times."

Emily finally glanced up at him. His eyes were full of compassion and kindness, like they always had been. She'd always loved the sparkle in his green eyes, and even the slight gap in his front teeth.

"Yes, like old times," she replied.

"Are you all right?"

He seemed to be drinking in the sight of her face.

She longed to reach out and touch his hand or his arm, any connection that might tell her if the spark that had always been remained, but it wouldn't be right.

"Honestly. . ." she trailed off.

It wouldn't do to fall to pieces in front of him. "I'm quite fine. Thank you for asking."

As she took the next step to walk past him, the air shifted and her heart squeezed. His eyes seemed to ask her to stay, but she broke away from the gaze and hurried up the stairs.

She blew out a relieved but amazed breath. The spark was definitely still there. For her, anyway.

Anna's bedroom door was ajar, and she could hear soft voices behind it. She knocked lightly, then joined them.

"We were hoping you would come," Anna said with delight.

Emily smiled. "You look beautiful."

The wedding gown was crisp white with intricate blue Celtic knots sewn in. The lace was tastefully gathered around the bodice and the hem. The long silk sleeves reached just past her wrists, making her look like an Irish princess of old. Her long brown hair was around her shoulders in curls and two braids wrapped across her crown with sprigs of holly mixed in.

"Doesn't she?" June chimed in. "Oscar said the braids symbolize feminine power and luck in Irish tradition. But she won't wear my red lipstick no matter how much I try to convince her."

"She looks lovely precisely how she is," Emily said, her eyes getting misty. "I'm glad to have this moment with both of you."

Anna reached for her hands, and June put her arms around both their shoulders.

"This isn't how I imagined my life to go, but here we are," Emily said, trying to sound strong. "You both are so special to me."

Anna wiped a tear away with a smile.

"No tears for the bride," June said, a hand on her hip. "Let's freshen you up and get ready for the big event. It won't be a long affair, will it?"

"June!" Emily said, shocked by her candor, even though she shouldn't have been.

"Well, I'm only wondering," June said with a shrug.

Anna smiled. "Shouldn't be terribly long. I wanted to incorporate a couple of the traditions my parents had at their wedding, but Reverend Ellis isn't a long-winded fellow."

Emily peered out the window. The small group of people was migrating toward the lit candelabra and chairs. Ben and Levi stood near the house talking, and she sucked in her breath. Levi had grown significantly taller since their early years. All the childish fat around his face had vanished, and his sharp jaw looked handsome in the candlelight. She swallowed and turned to her friends as Oscar and Greta peeked in the door.

"You ready, lassie?" he asked, eyes twinkling. "You look quite like your mother at her wedding. It's uncanny."

Greta had tears glistening in her eyes, and she handed a linen handkerchief to Anna. "I wish I had fabric from the one your mother was given on her wedding day, but this is a special handkerchief my mother gave me long ago. I want you to have it."

Anna reached for the older woman and they embraced.

Emily excused herself, and June followed her out the door and down to the grass. The dark blue of twilight was already seeping into the sky, but the small fire pits and candles brought a warmth that kept the chill in the air mild.

She didn't want to sit up front with Greta, because she didn't want to watch Levi stealing glances at Elizabeth. As they moved toward June's family, she bumped into her boss, Mr. Grayson.

"Good to see you here, Emily," he said with a friendly nod. "I don't think you've met my wife yet. This is Peggy Sue. And my daughter—I believe you've met."

The two women had their backs turned in conversation but twirled around when they heard their names. It was Levi they were speaking with, and Emily blushed in spite of her best efforts.

Elizabeth slipped her hand around Levi's arm, smoothing her pink silk dress, which was covered by a crisp black cloak. "Wonderful to see you again, Emily."

"We expect our daughter to be married soon as well, don't we, Peggy Sue?" Mr. Grayson said loudly.

"Hush, dear, don't be vulgar," Peggy Sue replied, every bit as timid as her daughter.

"Well, Levi has been promoted to a manager position at Yesler's Mill, hasn't he? Soon he'll be invited to their fancy dinner parties, and he'll be making a solid, respectable income." He crossed his arms triumphantly, clearly proud of his soon-to-be son-in-law.

Levi was turning pink and looking at his feet. Emily only looked up at him once, but he didn't return the gaze. His silence made the conversation turn stiff, so she took the opportunity to leave.

"Good to see you all, and nice to meet you, Mrs. Grayson," she said, then spun around to find June.

Heart racing and her self-confidence completely shattered,

she and June found her family settled on a quilt while baby Joseph slept away in his basket. Dr. Evans greeted them both, making space for them on the quilt.

"Right on time, ladies," he said. "How's the bride?"

"She's perfect and ready," June said with a grin. "I better get on up there."

Emily waved as her friend walked away. She was glad Anna had asked her to stand up with her for the ceremony, but she didn't want any more attention than absolutely necessary.

The sound of a lone cello playing a waltz drifted toward her, reminding her of her own wedding, but she pushed the thought away. Only another hour longer and she could slip away without being noticed. Once they said their vows, no one would detect her absence.

Anna and her grandfather emerged from the house, and a collective sigh came over the crowd. She truly looked stunning, cloaked in white wool and lace with the soft winter mist rising behind her.

The bride was beaming, her eyes trained on Ben down the aisle. Emily avoided looking in that direction so as not to see the same look Ben had in his eye in Levi's as he looked over at Elizabeth, perhaps imagining this day for them in the coming months.

Now the night seemed almost warm with all the bodies crowded together, hugging the tree line. There were also two fire pits on either side of the sitting places, which made it all the warmer.

When Anna and her grandfather reached the front, he gave her hand to Ben, then sat on a wooden chair next to Greta. The reverend began his words, voice booming. He wrapped a blue ribbon around the hands of the bridal couple over and over again in a figure eight as he spoke. The infinity symbol, Emily supposed. That was something she hadn't done at her own wedding, and she hadn't been to many others.

Then Ben began to speak in a low voice, quiet at first and then louder as he turned toward the audience, his eyes still trained on Anna.

". . .I love thee to the depth and breadth and height my soul can reach, when feeling out of sight for the ends of being an ideal grace. I love thee to the level of every day's most quiet need, by sun and candlelight. . ."

His words were vaguely familiar. It was an Elizabeth Barrett Browning poem she'd heard before. Without thinking, her eyes wandered over to Levi and their gazes locked. Her heart jumped with such fierceness it made her chest ache. How long had he been watching her?

His eyes were apologetic.

Does he feel sorry for me?

But his look said more than that. It was as if he were asking her something—something important.

She smoothed her skirts in front of her, noticing how short she had bitten her fingernails. It was certainly unseemly.

Looking back up at him, finding his eyes still on her, the realization came: perhaps he was thinking of a life with her.

Surely, she was seeing things. Startled, she looked away again.

The rest of the ceremony blurred together as her heart pounded with hope. Maybe he still thought of her—still dreamt of sharing his life with her.

It was too much to hope for, but she had nothing else to cling to. Life kept tossing impossible waves at her, and the warm look in his eyes was a harbor in the storm. Even if the gaze had been without meaning, even if he had no plans to put action behind the promise in his look, she would cling to that hope with all her strength.

She was lost in thought and staring at her hands when the sound of chiming bells filled the air around her. Anna and Ben, grinning widely, made their way down the makeshift aisle between wooden chairs and blankets.

Emily stood, grabbing baby Joseph out of his basket for a distraction. He cooed and looked up at her with big blue eyes. They were dark blue, perhaps turning hazel like June's. The baby wrapped his tight fist around one of her fingers, which brought her peace for the first time since she'd arrived at the wedding.

Everyone moved toward the house for the feast. Dr. Evans picked up the basket and quilt they'd been sitting on and gathered June from the front. Emily was grateful neither of them minded that she held on to Joseph a little longer. At six months old, he still smelled so new. With that creamy skin and milky breath, he was like a new beginning.

After most of the guests had gone inside, she stood with the baby wrapped in a quilt, watching the deep blue take over the winter sky. Stars began to poke through, and she pointed out each one to Joseph, who stared wide-eyed. He probably couldn't see them and was only amusing her, but she loved the feeling of teaching him something, helping him discover something new.

The thought of going inside the house made her stomach twist. The tables had turned on her and Levi's economic statuses, and the irony felt cruel. She had accepted her former marriage for the privileges it offered, hoping one day their love would materialize into something intimate. Perhaps it would have one day, but now she'd never know.

Exasperated, she told herself the choice had been made

with a right mind. Her feelings were secondary, as they should have been in order to secure safety, society, and a proper home. She had little power other than to create a life for herself and make sure her mother was taken care of as she aged.

June stepped out of the house at just the right moment. "How are you? You know you don't have to stay, right?"

Emily wiped away the tears that wet her cheeks. She handed the baby back to his mother, careful to keep the quilt wrapped tightly around him, even though he'd been as warm as a hearth in her arms.

"Yes, thank you for coming out here. I should be going." She took a deep breath and looked into June's eyes.

"It's not too late, ya know." June nuzzled Joseph's cheek, a content look on her face. "For you and Levi."

Emily looked around to make sure no one had heard. "It is though. It's genuinely too late now, and it's all my fault. I deserve this."

June frowned with a doubtful look on her face. "And I deserved to be a prostitute? I don't believe in that—*deserving* things. But I do know everything can change on any given day. So you need to have hope, all right?"

Emily kissed her friend's cheek and whirled away, unable to answer her optimistic words. There was nothing to be said—at least nothing she believed was true.

CHAPTER FOURTEEN

BY THE ROOTS

ANNA | *FEBRUARY 1891*

Anna awoke in the dark and rolled over to see Ben sleeping peacefully. She slipped out of bed and padded down the stairs to her favorite spot in the house—the bay windows that faced the mountain. The only thing visible in the dark winter morning was a full moon and a couple lasting stars.

She stoked the fire and added a few more logs, then curled up on one of the wooden chairs made by her grandfather. It would have been nice to have Esther crawl up into her lap and begin purring. That was one of the many things she missed from her childhood life, but living with Ben was far better in most respects.

The large bookshelves on either side of the fancy fireplace with its dark mantel was another aspect of the house she loved. She'd been busy reading *Anna Karenina* and *A Lady's Life in the Rocky Mountains* and she hadn't had much time to pick up any of the other titles Ben had purchased for them, especially since most of their free time was spent training.

She and Ben had written letters to finalize their spot on the team and read through John Muir's 1888 account. They also discovered one written by A.C. Warner, the photographer who'd climbed with Muir. And finally, they had come up with a careful plan to get their bodies and lungs in ideal shape for climbing come August.

She looked up at the brick fireplace as the flames began to crackle and grow, producing a comforting warmth in the cozy room. It brought a smile to her face thinking of Ben's proposal, and she eyed the brick in the bottom right corner of the fireplace that had a small mountain drawn on it. It was where he'd hidden her ring, which she now twisted around her finger absentmindedly.

It was a Sunday morning and one of the only chances Ben had to sleep in, but it was also the day she planned to visit Kiyotsa. She hoped he would wake before she left.

After reading a few chapters of *Anna Karenina*, she moved toward the kitchen to make breakfast with Dolly's words ringing in her ears.

When you love someone, you love the whole person just as he or she is, and not as you would like them to be.

Words Tolstoy had written over a decade prior, and they still applied in 1891.

Married life with Ben had been nearly as blissful as she'd imagined, but of course there were little things that surprised her and other things they disagreed on.

Ben's parents had left the morning after the wedding somewhat abruptly. Anna was actually glad to see them go.

The thought of his father now made her uncomfortable. Nevertheless, she was glad Ben had reconciled with his parents in time for the ceremony. The wedding had been as lovely as she'd imagined, and married life with Ben was more than she could have hoped for.

As she was cracking the eggs, she heard her husband come up behind her. He kissed her cheek and wrapped his arms around her waist as she worked.

"Good morning," he said sleepily.

"I worried you might not wake before I left."

"Ah, that's right. You're off to visit Heather's grandmother. I'm sure she'll be over the moon to see you. And Heather won't return for another couple weeks, right?"

Anna nodded, then flipped the eggs with a wooden spatula. "It's exactly when I promised her I'd go, and I think it'll be a lovely day."

She dished up plates for both of them while he poured two cups of coffee and brought them to the polished cedar dining table.

"Would you like to come along?"

Ben frowned. "I was hoping to catch up on some reading today and rest my back before heading to the mill again tomorrow. I only have a few chapters left of *Frankenstein*."

She was disappointed, even though the plan all along was that she'd go by herself. "That's fine, of course."

It would have been wonderful if he'd wanted to join her, but it wouldn't make either of them happy if she insisted on it. Unless he was hoping for her to press the issue? Sometimes married life was confusing. She decided not to overthink it and instead enjoy the breakfast.

After they'd eaten and washed the dishes clean, she packed a few things, kissed Ben good-bye, and set out into the forest. It would be good to have a full day to visit with Kiyotsa and help with any chores.

The sparrows and warblers called out from their winter roosts while squirrels scurried past her. The refreshing scent of fir needles and sap greeted her, along with the mossy musk she knew so well. She thought of when Ben had taught her to shoot, right inside the forest beyond the Gallagher backyard. It had been the first time in her life she'd been so attracted to a man and had also wanted to talk with him for hours on end.

During her walk, she reminisced about the wedding and the sound the small bells had made as she and Ben walked away as a married couple. That night at the Occidental Hotel had been magical, and they'd stayed up all night marveling in the pleasures that married life brought. But the time had gone quickly, and she couldn't wait until their spring honeymoon. It would be full of camping under the stars, walking through the forest, and kissing the most handsome man on earth.

And then, there would be the mountain. Come August, she and Ben would head south as a joint force to be reckoned with and perhaps summit Mount Rainier. If they succeeded, it would feel as if she overcame something inside herself—to know she was capable.

This time, she wouldn't be surprised by the bright glare of the sun off the mountain, how ice-cold the nights were, and how easy it was to slip toward the edge of a crevasse. She would be stronger, more experienced, and make sure to enjoy every moment of the climb.

Mr. Flannaghan had said there was a warm spring of water in the crater at the top. And that would be the reward for pushing her body and will to the edge—putting her tired feet in a hot spring at the tallest spot in her world. And it would be a luxurious bonus that Ben would be beside her, appreciating her strength and loving her just the way she was.

By the time she reached Heather's house, the cool air had warmed up to that of a mild winter's day. Heat radiated inside her torso from the pace she'd kept on the way, and she looked forward to taking off her hat and coat inside. Kiyotsa probably had something like stewed jack rabbit and dumplings cooking. Just the thought made her tummy rumble.

She knocked on the wooden door, then pushed it open slowly so as not to scare the woman. There was a strange smell, and Kiyotsa was nowhere to be seen. There was no fire and everything was tidy.

But when her eyes moved toward the bed, she saw her. Anna rushed to the bedside and put a hand on Kiyotsa's shoulder. It was still and cold.

Panic gripped her. She shook the old woman's shoulders, but there was no life left in her.

She should have visited sooner. When had Heather asked her to come? It was early February, Anna was sure of it.

Kiyotsa was certainly capable of taking care of herself, even through a mild winter.

Tears spilled down her cheeks as she accepted the finality of the life expired. Had she simply died of old age?

Anna inspected the cabin, looking for any sign of illness or hunger. There was a basket of moldy flatbread on the kitchen table and various jars of blackberries and strawberries near the cookstove. Dried meat was wrapped in a cloth nearby. At least she hadn't died from starvation, which would have been an insufferable truth—something Anna couldn't have lived with. It would have been unlikely anyhow, but she was grateful for the clear evidence.

If the old woman had fallen ill, it would have been while

isolated, and there probably wouldn't have been much a doctor could have done to help her. Kiyotsa had been excellent with dried herbs and different natural remedies from the forest.

It looked as if she had made a batch of flatbread for the next day, tidied up the cabin, and then gone to sleep for the evening, tucked comfortably in her bed under the quilt. Most likely, the woman had died peacefully in her sleep, and she was far older than any person Anna had known.

But the fact that Heather didn't know of her grandmother's passing sent a jolt of alarm through her. Judging by the pungent smell in the cabin and the amount of decay in the flatbread, the death had probably happened sometime in the last week. Luckily, the winter temperatures had kept her mostly preserved. And since the cabin had been secured, no animals had stolen in to disturb her eternal sleep.

She couldn't let Heather return to this though. Should she bury Kiyotsa before Heather and Pisha returned? How did the Duwamish honor their dead?

She then remembered how Heather had buried Dmitri and marked a small grave for him.

She escaped the cabin for fresh air and to find the site. She could leave now and return the next day with Ben to help dig the grave in the cold ground. But she couldn't bring herself to leave Kiyotsa out here alone, especially knowing she'd been on her own when she died.

No, she'd do the work herself, say some words for her friend, and mark the grave in a special way so Heather would know that her grandmother had been treated with dignity upon her death.

She found a shovel near the garden and searched for

Dmitri's grave. After some time, she identified the area marked with a large rock and covered in wildflowers.

Anna got to work digging into the ground. The top layers were dead leaves and branches, then she hit cold earth. The last layer would have been nearly impossible to budge if it hadn't been for the moderate weather in recent days.

By the time she'd unearthed a large enough area to bury the woman, hints of twilight were creeping up the sky. The mindless digging had taken her hours. She'd have to spend the night at the cabin, but she'd better get Kiyotsa in the ground first.

She rolled the body onto its side, surprised by how rigid it was, then rolled it into the quilt. She could drag the body that way, but it would be nearly as slow as digging the grave had been. She was thankful for the strength and the training that made her capable of the work that had to be done.

By the time she had Kiyotsa in her grave and covered with fresh dirt, night had fallen. It was cold, but her work had made her warm.

She sat down next to the grave. "Kiyotsa, you were a wonderful woman. Heather and Pisha loved you dearly, and I did too. Thank you for looking out for me in all the little ways you did. I'm especially grateful for how you helped June bring her baby into the world. I don't think Heather and I could have gotten through that without you."

She paused, and the cold dirt beneath her began to chill her as her body temperature cooled down.

"I know your own husband died a long time ago, but I expect that wherever you're going now, he'll be there waiting for you."

With that, she nodded once, stood, and returned to the cabin. Inside, she started a fire with the wood stacked near the hearth, something she probably should have done earlier. But it had been good to keep the door open to air out the smell of decay. She took the moldy flatbread off the table and brought it outside where the animals would likely find it. If they rejected it too, it could turn to dirt where it lay.

When she was finally finished, she sat down in front of the fire, wondering if she was more tired than she was hungry.

A twig cracked outside the cabin, and she froze. There was something particularly spooky about being all alone in the woods at night after dragging a dead body outside to bury it. But the sensation of another soul nearby rivaled any fear she might have had before.

When the iron latch of the cabin door rattled, she reached for the ax near the firewood and stood quickly.

But she recognized Ben's figure at once and ran to him, ax still in hand.

"I was worried when you weren't home by nightfall," he said. "You usually make it back pretty quickly."

Anna began to cry. "It's Kiyotsa. She's dead."

He wrapped her up in an embrace, stroking her hair. "I'm sorry, Anna. I can dig a grave for her in the morning. Where is she now?"

She shook her head. "It's already done."

She sniffed and felt no pride at his surprised look, only sorrow for the death and how saddened Heather would be on her return home.

"Oh, Anna, you could have come back, and I'd have helped you. Not because you couldn't do it on your own, but so you wouldn't be alone."

"I couldn't leave *her* alone," she said through her tears.

He nodded gravely and wiped a tear off her cheek. "It

looks like you have everything taken care of here. Were you planning to stay the night?"

"I'm completely exhausted."

"Have you eaten anything since you arrived?"

She shook her head. "There's food. I wasn't sure if I wanted any."

He released her and went to rummage around the kitchen, returning to her by the fire with some dried meat. "Let this tide you over until morning. I'll stay with you here tonight."

She ate quickly and then they curled up into Heather's bed. She was asleep in minutes.

The next morning, she woke to the sight of Ben bent over the fire making coffee.

"Good morning, dear," he said with amusement. "You must have worked hard last night because you rarely sleep this late."

Her shoulders and back were quite sore. She probably should have taken breaks between the digging and dragging, but she had also been racing the sun.

"I'd like to find wildflowers and plant them around her grave. And find a nice large rock to mark it as well."

"Yes, ma'am, but let's get some breakfast in you first."

She nodded and slipped out of the bed, wearing the dress she'd walked to the cabin in. It was gritty against her skin and lightly damp with sweat. Her dreams had been odd and slightly disturbing, and it had been a comfort to wake and have Ben near.

After a quick breakfast, she put her coat on to find wildflowers. Perhaps if she planted them around the grave, they would still be there for Heather to see them.

Ben chopped more firewood so it would be ready when Heather and Pisha returned.

Anna found some tiny purple and white pansies growing under the ferns of a nearby tree. She dug them out gently by the roots and then replanted them around Kiyotsa's final resting place. She was still there when Ben came to find her.

"Ready?" he asked softly.

"We should leave a note for Heather," she replied. "In case she comes back here first before stopping through town."

He nodded and waited while she returned to the cabin to scrawl on a page she had to rip out of a book. Hopefully, Heather would stop in town first. Surely, she wanted to see Michael before returning home. It would be far better to tell her in person, although Anna was dreading the responsibility.

CHAPTER FIFTEEN

BURN IT DOWN

ANNA

Two weeks later, Anna still thought of Kiyotsa every day. On her way to the bookstore one morning, she noticed all the winter flowers in bloom, some hiding under porches and some peeking behind stumps. She hoped that the ones she'd replanted over the woman's grave would still be alive when Heather returned. Even more than that, she hoped that Heather would stop through town first so she could tell her the terrible news before she had to find out the difficult way.

The bell above the door jingled as she entered the bookstore, and the immediate calming effect of the place relaxed her. Her grandfather was already there dusting bookshelves, even though they were always pristine. A vase of cinnamon sticks and pussy willows sat at the counter, making the air smell rich and inviting.

"Good morning, lassie. I'm looking through a new

catalogue. Have you heard of Oscar Wilde's new novel *The Picture of Dorian Gray*?"

She hung her shawl on a hook near the door. "I haven't. When is it available?"

"In April. It was published in a shorter version this past July in Lippincott's Monthly Magazine, but it'll be available soon as the full-length novel." He puffed on his pipe and pointed toward the listing. "It seems to be quite philosophical and controversial. You may like it."

She laughed. "I'm not exactly trying to push the boundaries about everything in the world."

"Only mountain climbing?" His eyes twinkled.

"I'm glad you can tease about it now, instead of threatening to disown me." She winked back at him.

They settled into their normal rhythm, greeting customers as they entered and helping them find the book they were looking for or the supplies they needed for stationary or school. Sometimes, they had to order books if they didn't have them in stock, and her grandfather usually took care of that. Anna enjoyed handling the money and keeping their financial affairs in order. She hoped they could always work together in this way, so enjoyably in a place that made her feel like she was home, even though she was at work.

"I think everything is mostly ready for the opening of the library in April," he said, joining her at the counter.

"I'm delighted they chose the space over the Occidental Hotel. Fifth floor, facing the new Pioneer Place Park—it's going to be dreamy," she said, putting her elbow on the counter and then resting her chin in her hand.

"I do hope it doesn't take too much business away from us."

She looked at him thoughtfully. "I think we'll be fine.

Nothing is better than the pleasure of owning one's favorite book."

❧

A WEEK LATER, Anna opened her front door to find Heather on the porch, face tear-streaked and eyes bloodshot. She was panting as if she'd run the whole way from the cabin.

When Anna reached out to her, Heather put her hand up and shook her head.

"Not yet. Tell me what happened."

"I'm so sorry, Heather," she said, biting her lip with more guilt than she should. "I went out to visit in early February like you asked. I should have gone sooner——"

"How did you find her?" Heather asked, looking at the ground.

"She was in her bed. It looked like she had simply gone to sleep for the night and. . .never woke up."

Heather covered her face with her hands and began to sob. Anna tried again to reach out to her friend, and this time Heather let her.

"But I should have gone sooner, and I'm sorry." She wrapped her arms around Heather's shoulders, an aching thickness in her throat.

"I never should have left her," Heather said, sinking into a dining room chair.

"Where's Pisha?"

Heather wiped her tears with the back of her hand. "She wanted to stay the night with Michael in town while I got everything settled back at home."

Anna nodded. "Let's get you tea, and then I'll head back to the cabin with you——"

"No, let's go now. Show me where you buried her."
Heather stood and marched toward the door.

Anna scrambled to get her boots and coat before following
her out the door.

The forest was thick with undergrowth. Dark clouds began
to cover the sky, and she wondered if the weather might clear
up for their planned honeymoon beginning that weekend. But
soon, clouds descended and rain poured. Streams of water
cascaded down on her from the ends of branches. Water
pooled in the toes of her boots, soaking her thin stockings. The
air had chilled when the clouds rolled in from the sea, and the
cool wind, the shade from the trees, and her wet clothing
chilled her.

It was hard to talk to Heather with the thundering patter
of rain falling on trees, leaves, and logs. Heather was still
crying as she walked, and Anna wasn't sure how best to
comfort her.

When they finally arrived, she was soaked through her coat
and boots.

"Where is she?" Heather asked, her voice loud over the
rain and howling wind.

Anna pointed and then began to walk toward Kiyotsa's
grave. When she found it, Heather slumped in front of it and
finally stopped crying.

Anna wiped the rain from her face and squeezed it out of
her braid. She ought to start a fire so they could warm
themselves, but she didn't want to leave Heather alone. Not
yet, anyway.

After a few minutes, Heather stood and inched toward the
garden. Anna walked up to the porch of the cabin and sat
down under the awning where they found some protection
from the torrential downpour.

Heather leaned down and surveyed the winter crops. Kiyotsa had left carrots, parsnips, and onions in the ground to keep through the winter. There were also sturdy bushes of rosemary and thyme along the wooden garden fence.

She leaned down and pulled up a few carrots. Then she kneeled and began ripping out anything she could get her hands on.

Anna stood and rushed over to her. "What are you doing?"

Heather didn't even look up, but her eyes filled with tears. She lunged at the herbs, tearing them out at their roots and tossing them as far as she could into the forest.

Anna grabbed both of Heather's hands. "Stop!"

"I can't stay here, Anna," she said between sobs. "I never want to see this place again."

"But Kiyotsa's here——"

"She's gone."

Heather turned toward the cabin, and Anna followed her inside.

They both stripped down to their undergarments and started a fire. Shivering from the cold, Anna wrung out their coats and dresses, hung them on a line by the fire, and began to boil water.

Heather rummaged around the cabin, apparently packing her and Pisha's things.

Anna wasn't sure if she should try and talk her out of this now or later. Either way, Heather needed to eat something.

After serving grits with preserved strawberries and hot tea, Heather curled up in her bed. All the crying and running and tearing apart the garden must have exhausted her because she was asleep in minutes.

Anna rocked in Kiyotsa's chair by the fire, watching through the window as the rain stopped and a few rays of light poked through the trees. She stayed that way until Heather stirred an hour later. She stood stiffly and joined her near the fire, silently unpinning her dress from the line.

"We should be going. Looks like the rain has let up." Heather pulled her dress over her head, nodding toward the window.

Anna dressed as well. "Should I put the fire out? Or will you be coming back this evening?"

"You can burn the place down. I don't care." Heather reached for the bag she'd packed before sleeping, then marched toward the door.

❦

THE NEXT DAY, as Anna walked out of the bookstore, she found a small white juniper flower along the street to put behind her ear. Then she made her way toward the restaurant to meet Ben for dinner after his last shift of the week.

When she arrived, he was already inside and seated at a table, and it was barely a quarter until six. She hurried inside to join him.

"Good evening," she said.

He stood up from his seat to greet her with a small bow. "My love. I already ordered, and the food should be here soon."

"Awfully presumptuous of you," she said with mock offense. "Did you get a chance to speak with Michael today at the mill?"

"I hope you wanted ice cream for dinner. . ." Ben trailed off intentionally, then grinned. "Not yet, but I plan to go over there tonight. Maybe take him out for a drink so we can speak privately."

"She says she's going to move into town and finally live with him," she said with a frown.

"But isn't that a good thing to come of this?" Ben asked, nodding kindly at the waiter as he set their plates in front of them.

"She's unhappy though. I can't tell if she's angry with me or at herself. I don't think she's grieving in the best way."

"Everyone grieves differently. Maybe she needs solitude. I'll definitely speak with Michael tonight and make sure everything is all right."

Anna sighed, putting her napkin on her lap. "Our honeymoon can't come soon enough. We need some time off. Time away."

"I can't wait to have you all to myself under the stars," he said with a wink that made her blush.

"Did anyone at the mill make a fuss about you requesting a whole week off in April?"

"They weren't overjoyed about it, but Levi's going to fill in for me when needed," he said. "And I would have just found a different job if they wanted to fire me over it."

She smiled coyly. "You're sounding quite confident in yourself, darling."

"It's only because I have your love, so I have all I need," he said, as their steaming hot baked spareribs arrived.

CHAPTER SIXTEEN
SPRING RAIN

EMILY | APRIL 1891

I n early April, Emily began to come back to life. Her appetite had returned, and her work at the grocer had become a welcome habit. She donned her apron as she began her shift, then dug the metal scooper into the dried beans to measure out a bag that had been ordered the evening before.

Elizabeth had left to visit her aunt in Oregon to help with the many children and the spring planting, so there was little chance of bumping into Levi at the store.

The bell jingled over the front door, and she looked up to see Greta Gallagher.

"Good morning, Greta," she said with a grin. "How nice to see you this morning. What can I get for you?"

"I'd like sugar and salt, but, in truth, I came here to invite you over for dinner, dear." She leaned up against the counter and rested her elbows on top.

Emily reached behind her for a large bag of salt. "How many pounds of salt?"

It was common for her to receive pity dinner invitations. She mostly refused them. Everyone wanted to take care of the widow by feeding her, and it was too depressing. But the Gallaghers were like family to her, and Levi's fishing boat would have already left for the spring fishing season.

"I'll take one pound, please," Greta said, a twinkle in her eye.

"Yes, that sounds nice. I'd love to join you. What day did you have in mind?"

"Why, today."

"I haven't seen Anna in a couple weeks, so I'd love to catch up with her as well," Emily said, closing up the brown bag she'd put the salt into.

"Oh, Anna and Ben have dinner plans this evening," Greta said, looking around at the shelves. "But I'm making your favorite tonight—chicken pie with gravy—so I simply had to invite you."

Anna's absence certainly changed Emily's desire to go to the dinner, but how could she refuse now? "Oh, all right. Just the two of you? Shall I bring anything?"

Greta stood silently for a moment as if pondering something. "I'll take two pounds of sugar, dear. No, of course you don't need to bring anything."

Emily frowned and pulled out the silver scooper to get sugar from the bag.

As she took the coins from Greta and handed her the two brown bags of goods, she had an ominous feeling about the invitation.

But that evening, she arrived at the Gallagher home with a basket of biscuits her mother had made that morning. She'd been raised better than to arrive empty-handed, and Greta knew it.

As she knocked on the door, the clouds began to sprinkle. Thank goodness she'd already made it there dry. The rains were fickle in April, and it might very well rain on her all the way home, but at least she wasn't arriving as a sopping wet guest.

Greta opened the door and a gust of wind pushed against her back, guiding Emily inside the warm house. She took off her shawl and hung it up near the door, then gave Greta a hug.

"Thanks for inviting me over. I'm looking forward to—"

She stopped short as Levi emerged from the living room. Her heart squeezed, and she instinctively backed toward the door, but he seemed as surprised as she was.

"Emily," he said, standing taller and clearing his throat.

"I was sure you'd be gone on your fishing trip," she said, crossing her arms over her chest and trying to disappear. "At least, this is around the time you used to go."

"Yes, Captain Pavitt came through last week. I don't actually need to go on fishing trips anymore since—" He paused, shuffling his feet. "I'm a manager now at the mill, so I can't leave for months on end like I did when I was younger. Plus, it was difficult work for a little cash and some halibut."

"Well, now you can buy it from your friends when they come through again," Greta said happily. "And you can go fishing around here any weekend you like."

Levi blushed, but his chest puffed out a little at her words.

He probably made a fine manager—fair and kind but realistic. And apparently they paid him well enough to skip his yearly fishing trip.

Greta must have planned this on purpose. The woman

beamed as she looked at the two of them. Emily sighed. There was no polite way to escape, so she moved toward the kitchen slowly.

"Will you visit Elizabeth at her aunt's house?" she asked Levi without looking up.

"I hadn't thought about it, but I suppose I could take the train down for a day or so." He drifted toward her, taking a seat opposite from her at the dining room table.

Greta excused herself back into the kitchen, and Emily found herself alone at the table with him.

He looked up at her sheepishly. "I had no idea she invited you over——"

"Clearly." At first, she wanted to scowl, but she laughed instead.

Levi grinned when she laughed, seemingly relieved. "It's good to see you."

She cleared her throat. "It is. I hope it's not too. . .strange for you since. . .you're courting Elizabeth."

"Don't worry. I won't beg you to marry me again," he said with a playful smile.

The gap between his front teeth had always been endearing to her. It made him still seem like a boy in a way. But his frame was tall and lean, and his shoulders had broadened in the last couple of years.

She looked down at her hands and grew quiet, not meeting his gaze.

"I'm sorry. That was in poor taste." He leaned in on his elbows, his head tilted sideways. "How have you been?"

"No, it's fine. I deserve that."

"You don't. I was trying to be funny, I guess. I should have gone straight to asking you how you are. Do tell me, please?"

She sighed and looked up into his green eyes. She found

true acceptance there—not the disdain she'd always feared and expected after her rejection.

"I'm doing fine as of recently," she said honestly. "My work at Grayson's has kept me busy. I make nearly two dollars per week."

"It's ridiculous his debt fell to you," Levi said, concern in his eyes.

"Is it?" she asked, fire in her chest. "You've never quite understood how badly women have it. I'm a pawn, Levi, with no power and no rights. But I can certainly take blame and debt, can't I?"

"I'm sorry—"

"It doesn't matter how you feel about it. It's just the way of things. I've acted in my best interest with the choices I've made, and things still didn't work out for me. That's all right. Not your fault and not your problem. But it would be nice for you to acknowledge that my marrying Charles was a good move at the time."

"I'll never say that," he said, sitting back in his chair and crossing his arms.

A silence fell over them, and her heartbeat sped up.

"You're being stubborn," she said, eying him warily.

Levi lowered his voice. "I loved you, Em. The rest didn't matter."

Her skin tingled at the first sentiment but recoiled at the second. "How can you say that? You haven't the faintest idea what it's like to have no power."

"Not as a woman. That's true. But I've been the newest fisherman on a boat full of old men. And I've worked at the mill for years with no respect as a young man."

"It's not the same," she said, exasperated.

"I'm sorry," he replied earnestly. "I want to understand."

Was there truly any way he could know what it was like to choose stability over love, or financial security over happiness?

Oscar came down the stairs and seemed as surprised to see her as Levi had been.

"Hello, lassie," he said, recovering himself nicely. "I hope you're staying for dinner. Greta sure misses Anna, and she likes to have another gal around sometimes."

"Yes, I'm staying for dinner," she said, standing suddenly. "I should see if she needs any help in the kitchen."

She didn't glance at Levi as she left, but she knew exactly what his face looked like. She didn't know how to explain to him what it was like to be in her situation. If he couldn't understand, she didn't know how else to describe it.

In the kitchen, Greta was humming "Oh My Darling Clementine" over the cookstove and stirring something that smelled like garlic.

"Can I do anything to help?" Emily asked, leaning against the wall.

"You can chat with me, dear," Greta said, turning to look at her. "Tell me, how's your mother?"

"The winters are always hard on her, you know," she said, crossing her arms. "She's as well as to be expected."

"Glad to hear it. Did you get a moment to catch up with Levi?"

Emily tilted her head with a playfully accusing expression. "What are you up to, Greta?"

The older woman hefted a pie pan out of the oven, humming again. The thick crust was golden brown, the smell divine. "You all used to be such good friends. It's good for my heart to see you and June so close again. I don't think there's any harm in mending the friendship you and Levi once had. Might do your heart some good."

Greta placed the dinner biscuits Emily had brought in a basket, covered them with a cloth, and handed it to her. "Can you take these out for me? I'll be right out with the rest of it."

Emily sighed and nodded, not sure what to think of Greta's words. It did always bring her peace to be at the Gallagher house. She had wonderful memories of being a girl there, with hardly any cares, playing with dolls in the grass with Anna and June. And Levi taking them on long romps along the tree line, pretending to look for treasure. She smiled at the memories.

"Those smell delicious," Oscar said.

"Thank you. Well, I can't take the credit. My mother made them." She sat again across from Levi and looked up at him finally.

She recognized that look from the day of the wedding. A longing or sympathy—hard to tell which.

Oscar looked up at Levi. "Tell her about how you tried your hand at gold mining before you got locked in with the mill."

Greta arrived with the steaming pie and began to serve slices.

Levi shook his head and gave his grandfather an annoyed look. Then he sighed and took a large gold nugget out of his pocket, setting it on the table. "It was definitely an adventure. Made a little money, but I already spent it on my house. Though I kept this one for good luck."

"This is beautiful," Emily said, examining the nugget. "What are you planning on doing with it?"

"Probably keep it in my pocket and enjoy its shiny company," he joked, nodding at Greta as she served him the last slice. "In fact, I think I'll have it made into a watch. Or I'll sell it and put it into my house too."

She handed the nugget back to him. "You bought a house?"

"Yes," he replied, eyebrows raised thoughtfully. "It's an ordinary house near downtown."

"He's being modest," Greta added playfully, finally taking her seat. "It's a wonderful home. He's already found some choice pieces for the living room, and Oscar's helped him make some fine wooden chairs."

Emily smiled and looked down at the large piece of chicken pie Greta had served her. The fluffy yellow of the crust was buttered in the way she liked, but her stomach had turned uneasy.

After dinner, she put her shawl around her shoulders and thanked Greta for a lovely meal.

"You're welcome here anytime. You know that," Greta said with fondness.

"The rain is really coming down," Levi said, grabbing an umbrella. "Let me walk you down our road to the streetcar."

"I'll be quite all right walking home in the rain," she said, trying not to smile.

"Let me walk you, please," he said quietly. "I'd like to pay your way on the trolley."

"Yes, please take the trolley," Greta said. "At least that will get you across town, and maybe the rain will let up before you get near your house."

Emily acquiesced, giving Greta a hug. "Thanks again."

The rain came down in sheets, which it only ever did in spring, and she'd be soaked in seconds without an umbrella. Why hadn't she thought to bring one?

Levi opened his large black umbrella while they were under the awning of the porch and then put it over their heads. "Shall we?"

With one hand, he held the umbrella. The other, he offered to Emily.

She hesitated, not wanting to touch him and invite the old memories to come back. She thought of Elizabeth and propriety, and she shook her head.

"As you wish."

He started down the stairs slowly, and she followed closely under the protection of the umbrella.

The sound of raindrops hitting the oilcloth rang loud, and it would probably soak through in a few minutes. Long enough to get her down the road toward the trolley, which she didn't mind taking now after all. She had a few coins in her pocket, and no way would she let Levi pay her way.

"You're right. A woman's situation is much more complicated than being the new man on a fishing boat," Levi said, wiping his brow. "That was a strange comparison. I was only trying to empathize."

She believed him but didn't know what else to say. As she took her next step, her shoe stuck behind her in the mud. She stopped short, turning herself around to retrieve it.

Levi bent down to free the shoe from the mud. He looked as if he would help her put it back on, but then he seemed to think better of it and simply handed it to her.

She reached for the shoe and bent down to slip it back onto her foot. He offered his arm again. This time, she accepted.

His warmth felt so inviting that it almost took her breath away. She hadn't been on a man's arm since Charles had died, and she had forgotten how nice it was. Not only that, but being close to Levi made her heart race. She'd always loved him, and even if he couldn't understand her choices, she hadn't told him no because of a lack of desire.

They walked for a while in silence until they were nearly at the trolley station.

"I'll wait here with you until it comes," he said, planting his feet in the mud with deliberation, as if he expected her to argue.

"You don't need to take care of me," she said quietly. "I do appreciate your help, but I hope you don't feel obligated to take care of the poor widow."

He turned to face her, coming closer than she expected him to. "You will always be someone I want to take care of and have near."

Emily shook her head, confused. "Well, I'll be fine. The trolley will be here soon, and—"

"That's not what I mean," he said, his voice low.

"But Elizabeth—"

"Tell me I have any chance with you, right now, and I'll mail her a letter at once breaking off our courtship."

Emily froze. They were the words she'd wanted to hear, but she didn't know exactly what to say. She started nodding slowly.

Levi's eyes searched hers. "Yes? There's a chance?"

"Yes," she said, her eyes misting.

"I'd really like to kiss you, but I need to send that letter first." He cleared his throat and looked away.

She nodded, and the sound of the trolley became louder than the rainfall on their umbrella. Levi pulled coins from his coat pocket, but she shook her head.

"Let me pay." She wanted to embrace him but didn't. "Perhaps you can come by sometime next week after you send your letter."

He nodded a few times slowly, then took a deep breath, blowing it out away from them. "If it were any darker, I'd accompany you on the trolley, but I think you'll be home before nightfall."

He extended his hand as she moved to enter the trolley and she took it. A jolt of emotion shot through her like never before—with only a touch—something that had never once happened with Charles.

"Yes, I'll be fine," she managed to say and then let go of his hand reluctantly as she gained her footing on the streetcar.

Levi chewed his bottom lip and waved as the trolley took her away.

CHAPTER SEVENTEEN
THE LAST FEW PAGES

ANNA

"I have a surprise for you," Ben said, holding his hands behind his back.

It was the day before they were to leave for their honeymoon adventure under the stars, and Anna couldn't imagine what he might have behind him. He'd just arrived home from his last shift at the mill before being off for a whole week. His face was absolutely glowing with delight.

"Why did you get me a gift?" she asked. "Was I supposed to get you something?"

"Well, she's for both of us," he said, pulling a fluffy white and gray puppy from behind his back.

It let out a little ruff before looking up into Anna's eyes, melting her. The light blue puppy eyes matched the blue bow tied around its collar.

"Oh my!" she said, pulling the soft thing into her arms. "Where did you get it?"

"Friend of mine at the docks has a team of huskies up in Alaska. When I heard one of them was expecting, I told him we'd like one."

"She's a husky? Won't it be too hot for her here?"

"You don't like her?"

Ben looked stricken. He reached for the puppy, but she laughed and held it tight.

"I love her," she said, lifting it like a baby so they were face to face. She rubbed her nose against the puppy's wet one and knew she'd always needed a husky puppy in her life and never known it. "I don't know much about dogs though."

"Me either, but we'll learn together," he said, clearly relieved.

The day before leaving on their honeymoon did not seem like such a great time to take on the responsibility of a young puppy, but it didn't seem like much could be done about it now. Plus, it was absolutely darling.

"Shall we take her with us?" she asked, curling up with the pup on a chair.

"Of course." He sat down next to her, putting a hand on the puppy's head. "We're like a little family. What do you want to name her?"

"Would it be strange to name her Comma?"

"As in, the punctuation?" he asked, amused. "A little odd, yes."

Anna shrugged. "Well, I still like it."

He stood to his feet with excitement. "All right, Comma is fine. It's like we have a baby, right?"

"I guess so." She laughed. "I need to get ready for this evening. Would you like to join me, sweet puppy?"

Comma responded by arranging her eyebrows in the adorably questioning way only a dog can.

"I'd like to join you," Ben said, moving toward her suggestively.

She leaned toward him, planting a kiss on his lips. "But if we simply luxuriate in wedded bliss, we'll miss the ribbon cutting for the library."

"I'm fine with that," he said, eyebrows raised in question.

"But it's so enchanting that it's on the fifth floor of the Occidental Hotel." She started walking up the stairs, but not before scooping Comma into her arms. "And besides, our actual honeymoon starts tomorrow, so I think we'll have plenty of time. . .to be with each other."

"Well, I'll never be able to think of that hotel in the same way after spending our first night as a married couple there." He cleared his throat and started back toward the kitchen. "I'll be thinking about it the whole time we're there, just so you know."

Anna blushed and shook her head. Comma's fur was soft against her neck, and she ran her fingers along the puppy's soft paws. Walking up the stairs was apparently enough to lull the little thing to sleep.

When she got up to the bedroom they shared, she placed the puppy carefully on the white quilt. Her armoire was filled with all the clothes she'd brought from home when she'd moved in four months ago.

At first, the house had felt more like a vacation than a home. It was fancier than her childhood house, and nearly everything inside was new. Fresh paint, new furniture, and the kitchen table still smelled of cedar, like Ben sometimes did. The books that lined the walls on either side of the fireplace made her smile every time she walked by. And the bay windows that looked toward the mountain were still breathtaking.

The winter months since she'd lived there brought more low-hanging clouds than any other time of year, and the mountain was often obscured. If it wasn't smoke from the mills, it was a maritime cloud layer. But every once in a while, it all lifted and the dark blue sky made the white top of the mountain stand out beautifully.

She placed her mother's cameo pin at her collar and changed into a full royal blue skirt with layers of fabric that cascaded down with ribbons along each hem. Her French braid had begun to fall out in chunks, so she brushed her long brown hair until it shone, then she wound it up as best she could. Greta had always helped her do her hair for events for as long as she could remember, but doing it herself would have to do.

When a sharp whine sounded behind her, she spun around to see Comma digging with both large paws at the maroon and gold rug in the bedroom.

"No!" She rushed over and scooped her up. "Perhaps Ben should take you on a walk while I get ready."

❦

ANNA ROLLED over inside the tent to find Ben snoring beside her and Comma curled up at their feet. It was the third day of their honeymoon, and she never wanted to return to real life. Couldn't they live like this forever? Under the stars, surrounded by tall evergreen trees, in each other's arms?

The opening of the Seattle Public Library had gone off without a hitch. It actually ended up being quite uneventful. A vice president from a lumber mill that competed with Yesler's borrowed the first book: Mark Twain's *Innocents Abroad*. Then they had slipped out and back home, and she blushed at the memory.

She snuck out of the tent, hoping to get the fire going before he woke. Comma immediately awoke and followed her out.

She gathered sticks and a few logs they'd already set next to their makeshift fire spot. Once the fire was going, she pulled out the blank book he had given her the day he'd proposed. She had already filled some of the pages so far on their trip, and she couldn't wait to bring it up the mountain.

After she'd written a page or so describing the dark green canopy that surrounded them, she pulled out her copy of *Anna Karenina* and let Comma jump onto her lap for another snooze.

When Ben finally emerged from the tent, he came to sit down on the log beside her and cleared his throat. "Looks like you're about finished. How did you like it?"

She smiled.

"I enjoyed the story very much. Well, the ending is interesting. I think it all started going downhill when Anna and Vronsky ran off to Italy to be together. The ambiguity of her marriage bothered her and she seemed overly jealous."

He placed his hands on his knees and nodded. "Tell me more."

"I feel for her. She was powerful at the beginning and then faded to something smaller—more petty. Her brother had a much easier time with his affair. Seems to be the way of it no matter the year or the country. Men get away with things while women aren't granted the same rights."

"A harsh analysis, but you may be right. Tolstoy included lots of political undertones, and he certainly highlights the fact that Anna isn't treated the same as her male counterparts in regard to a number of issues."

"Have you finished *Frankenstein?*" she asked.

It was a book she had read the year prior and let Ben borrow. One of the few books she had that he hadn't already read.

"Sometimes, I think Dr. Evans might be doing the same thing as Dr. Frankenstein—piecing together a hideous creature from corpses." He looked at her sideways, trying to hide his smile.

"You'll need to start getting along with Connor at some point, you know," she said with a grin. "And Frankenstein's monster—that poor creature. He only wanted to find a friend."

"Actually, I think what he wanted most was acceptance from the one who created him," Ben said.

"Indeed," she said, closing the book in her lap.

There would be plenty of time to read the last few pages of the book in the afternoon, but they had hiking to do. Comma very much enjoyed long walks in the cool forest, which worked out perfectly. When they stopped to rest or eat, she would dig holes in the ground and curl up in the dead leaves and ferns for a nap.

It would be difficult to leave her when they left on their expedition, but she certainly couldn't come with them, not even to base camp. Anna also needed to figure out who might be able to watch the puppy while they were gone. Would Heather be up for the challenge?

CHAPTER EIGHTEEN

SHEER JOY

EMILY

A horse-drawn carriage pulled up in front of Emily's house, and she hoped it would be Levi. When he stepped out of the coach wearing a crisp suit and a top hat, she giggled in spite of herself. She rushed down the stairs and found her mother sitting at the table peeling potatoes absentmindedly.

"Who on earth could that gentleman be?" she asked, straining to see out the single-pane window in their house.

"It's Levi," she said, swinging the door open. Then she paused at the doorway, uncertain if she should run to meet him.

When he arrived at the door, his green eyes sparkled and he grinned widely. "Good evening, Emily. Mrs. Taylor. Is Mr. Taylor home?"

"He's out back with the cow," her mother said, looking

from him to her with confusion. "And you should call me Linda now. You're a full-grown man."

Emily hadn't yet mentioned anything to her mother. It was all too good to be true, and she didn't need any bad luck to come because she let it all out early. Plus, she didn't know for sure if Levi still felt the same as he had that night, or if he'd called off his courtship, although his presence gave a good indication.

He nodded importantly, taking off his hat. "I'll wait in here with you ladies, if that's all right. I'll speak with him when he returns."

"Of course," she said, breathless.

They all sat down at the wooden kitchen table.

"How is your courtship going, Levi?" her mother asked, beginning to peel potatoes again.

"In truth," he said, glancing at Emily with a secret smile, "things did not work out with Miss Grayson."

Emily's chest filled with warmth, and she couldn't stop smiling. Was this truly happening? After all these years?

He turned to her with a serious expression. "I posted a letter yesterday morning to Elizabeth. I spoke with her father this morning, and, for good measure, I also sent a telegram to her aunt's house. I want to do this right."

She nodded as her father came in the front door.

Levi stood. "Good evening, sir. Can I have a word with you?"

She held her breath while her father crossed his arms. In his mind, Levi had acted sweet on his daughter and then promptly disappeared from her life. She hadn't felt the need to explain things to him then, but now she would. Hopefully, he'd give Levi a chance in the meantime.

"Why don't we step out front?" her father said, seemingly unimpressed.

"Yes, sir." Levi hopped up and moved toward the door.

While they spoke outside, her mother put a hand on Emily's arm. "Is this what you want, Em? He's not much like Charles, is he?"

"No, he's not. And yes, this is exactly what I want. What I should have chosen years ago."

After a moment, her father stepped back in the house and motioned out the door. "This young man would like a word with you, Em. The choice is yours."

She rushed up to her father, kissing him on the cheek. "Thanks. I'll explain more later."

She shut the door behind her and walked with Levi toward his waiting carriage. The horses stomped their feet and swished their tails.

He reached for her hand but kept some distance between their bodies. "Emily, you've always been the one I wanted, more than anything else."

His palm was damp with sweat and warm to the touch. She wished she could pull it to her cheek or her chest, but her parents were watching through the window.

"I'm sorry I didn't choose you back then——"

"We don't have to dwell on the things that happened back then. This is our new start." He paused to clear his throat, a distant concern on his brow. "I'm a different man than the boy you shared so much with back then. I'd like to think I haven't changed all that much, but the truth is we both have. I'd like to spend time with you in the coming months so we can. . .reacquaint ourselves with each other. I think we owe that to ourselves."

She nodded, although apprehension crept up her throat.

Was it possible he wouldn't like the woman she'd become? What type of woman *had* she become? It was hard to know anymore—so much of her had been erased lately.

He was right. It was the new beginning she needed. Perhaps things wouldn't end in marriage for them, but it was absolutely worth a shot to see if the passion from their younger years might blossom into a real love to build a life on.

"Your father approved our courtship, although quite hesitantly, I might add," he said with confusion.

"I'll speak with him this evening. He doesn't quite have a clear picture of why our friendship soured."

"Ahh, indeed," he replied, relief flooding his features. "Well, if you'll have me, there's a dinner at Yesler's house this Saturday evening. There'll be a dance afterward, and I'd be delighted if you'd join me."

"I'd love to," she replied, feeling the blush come to her cheeks. "I'd love to be there with you."

She squeezed his hand, wishing she could do more. He tipped his hat slowly, meaningfully, then turned to get into the carriage. As it drove away, he put his hand out the window to wave at her like an excited little boy.

Emily laughed and waved back. She spun around to see both of her parents move quickly away from the window.

Inside, she was bombarded with questions.

"The main thing you need to know is I said yes to courting. We're going to a dance at the Yesler place this Friday, and, Father, it was me who turned him down all those years ago."

Her father cleared his throat. "Why?"

"Why did I say yes to courting him?"

"No. Why did you say no to him back then?" He folded his arms as if curiosity was getting the better of him.

"I can scarcely remember," she said.

Lying to her father made her feel guilty, but there was no point elaborating.

"Well, his face lights up like a sunbeam any time she walks in the room," her mother said. "Am I the only one who notices?"

Emily grinned and took a long drink of water.

"Levi's a good man," her father said. "But it seems like you have a complicated history."

"She's a grown woman and fully capable of deciding these things on her own, although I'm sure she appreciates your guidance, Rusty."

He gave her a dangerously serious look and shook his head. "This one decision will decide the rest of your life, Em. Don't choose wit and good looks over stability and success."

"That's what you said two years ago, and look where I am now," she said, exasperated.

She moved toward the stairs, thoroughly finished with the conversation, not looking back at her parents.

Her sister Lauren drifted out of her room where she'd been working on her embroidery. "What's gone on down there?"

"Levi is courting me, and he's taking me to a Yesler dinner this Friday."

"The Yesler Spring Dance? At their new mansion?" she asked, her eyes wide. "He has an invitation? It's all the talk right now."

"Is it really so exclusive?" Emily asked, suddenly concerned. Surely, Levi would have told her if this was a fancy, invitation-only event the whole town was talking about.

And then it occurred to her that he wouldn't have told her. He'd probably want it to be a delightful surprise for her.

"Yes, it is." Lauren put her hands on her hips, her lips pouty. "I wish I were old enough to be invited."

"You'll be neck-deep in this confusing world soon enough," Emily said, offering as much of a reassuring smile as she could manage.

"What will you wear?" Lauren asked.

That was certainly a concern. Maybe her mother could help her embellish a dress she already had, if this event was as extravagant as Lauren believed it was.

"Don't worry," Lauren said quickly. "We'll figure it out and you'll look stunning."

"Thanks." Emily gave her a quick hug and then escaped into her bedroom.

The setting sun threw a golden hue across her pale yellow quilt. She lay back onto the bed, trying to imagine the sheer joy of dancing with Levi. But the real delight would be spending the evening with her best friend.

CHAPTER NINETEEN

THE CARRIAGE SWAYED

EMILY

E mily powdered her face and chest while looking at her reflection in the mirror. Her mother had found pearl earrings for her to wear and a pearl barrette for her chignon. But first, she had to tame her unruly curls.

She'd never liked her curls—they were childish and completely unsophisticated.

Lauren entered the room, breathless. "I found little flowers for your hair."

"You're very sweet," she said, putting the powder away. "Thank you."

"A fine lady like you needs to look her best. And flowers in your hair are just the thing." Lauren laid a small bouquet of spring flowers on the dresser.

"You sound all grown up," she said, looking at her sister in the mirror. "When I left to get married, I could have sworn you were still wearing a pinafore."

"Well, now I'm in finishing school, and I'll be a lady soon," she said, a half-smile playing on her lips.

"I would have given anything to go to a finishing school," Emily said wistfully. "How lucky you are that one has started here in Seattle. Just in time for you."

Lauren curtsied with a playful grin on her face. "What can I say? I'm a lucky girl."

They both giggled as their mother opened the bedroom door behind them.

"It's wonderful to see you two together again under one roof. I fear it won't be for long though," her mother said, gliding into the room.

"Don't say such things," Emily said. "You know I don't need any bad luck at this point."

"You and your superstitions," her mother said with a dismissive tone. "That boy sure looked at you in a way I recognize. It's the way a man gazes at a woman when he's smitten."

He's always looked at me that way.

And it was downright endearing. Her stomach quivered when she thought of the evening ahead of her.

"He'll be here soon," she said, handing the brush to her mother. "Can you twist my hair up and put the pearl barrette in? You're the best at managing this mane."

Lauren laughed and excused herself while her mother went to work on her task. When she was finished, Emily was in awe.

"It's lovely," she said, reaching a finger up to touch her hair.

"No touching," her mother said softly. "This humidity will have your curls springing out in no time."

Emily stood as if she had a stack of books on her head. "I'm sure he'll be here soon. I better get dressed."

Her mother smiled, hesitating a moment while looking at her daughter. "I'm sorry I wasn't able to spruce up a dress for you. My hands have been so tender and painful lately."

"I know. It's fine." She looked down at her horrid nails and resigned herself not to worry too much about her appearance, although it was quite difficult.

"I did have a moment to stop in town to buy something for you though," her mother said with a twinkle in her eye.

"I certainly hope you're teasing," Emily said with surprise. "We don't have the money for surprises."

"I've been saving up for something special. When I saw your eyes light up again for the first time in a long time, Em, I knew this was without a doubt what I wanted to spend my money on."

Tears brimmed in her mother's beautiful brown eyes, then she motioned for Lauren to enter the room. She was holding the most magnificent dress Emily had ever seen.

"I don't believe it!" Emily stammered, her breath hitching in her throat.

The dress was made of purple satin with a lusciously layered bustle. Black beads hung like icicles along the capped sleeves, which would hide the skinniness of her arms wonderfully.

"I helped pick it out," Lauren said, beaming.

Emily hugged her mother first and then her sister. "It's too much. I'll feel like true royalty tonight. I'm incredibly grateful."

Her mother kissed her cheek. "I worried you might never light up again, but tonight, on Levi's arm, you will dazzle everyone with your sheer happiness. It's more than enough to delight me."

They helped her into the beloved dress, her mother lovingly buttoning each small pearl that closed the back as if she were preparing her for a wedding.

When Emily was dressed, they left her alone to make the final adjustments and gather herself. In the mirror, a beautiful, elegant woman looked back at her, and the joy radiating from her eyes was certainly there, as her mother had predicted.

She descended the stairs as gracefully as she could remember how. It had been quite a long time since she'd been to any important event, let alone with someone she couldn't stop thinking about. It was a whole new level of nerves, knowing Levi's every move affected her.

When the carriage pulled up, she could think of nothing but him. He stepped out like the happiest man in the world.

He froze as he caught sight of her, his jaw going slack so that a flash of his teeth showed.

"You look. . ." he stammered. "You're beautiful."

Emily could feel the blush on her cheeks, but she didn't care. She took the arm he offered and the electricity from his touch made the moment all the more exhilarating.

He looked as handsome as she'd ever seen him, but she was afraid if she opened her mouth to say so, she might cry from happiness.

Her mother and father wished her well, and Lauren was blowing her kisses as they walked out the front door together.

Levi offered his hand, and she gladly took it. His warmth reached through her white gloves. Inside the carriage, she rested her back against the cushioned seat, careful not to disturb her unpredictable chignon.

"You're breathtaking," he said, leaning forward in his seat. "I'm glad I'll have you to talk with at this thing tonight."

"I hear it's quite the event," she replied, a hint of scolding in her tone. "You could have told me this dance was the talk of the town."

He shrugged good-naturedly. "I guess I wanted to impress you. I know it's the type of event I used to tease you for wanting to go to."

There had been great hope and expectation in her heart back then. She'd imagined being madly in love with the man that took her to fine events. But even with as many fancy dinners and dances as she'd been to in the last year, she was certain she'd never been as adored as she was in this moment.

"Well, I'm spellbound," she said, gazing back at him.

Outside the small window of the carriage, the sun shone brightly, a rare occurrence for early April. The showers that had been unrelenting were finally turning to fairer skies. The high clouds looked wispy and unassuming, and they made her delightfully happy. Or perhaps it was this moment with Levi.

"I hope I don't embarrass you," he said, clearing his throat.

"How so?" she asked.

"I don't want to say the wrong thing or do something unsophisticated to make you cringe. This is your world."

She shook her head emphatically. "I'm thrilled to be here with you, but if you wanted to ignore the event completely and head to a rocky beach to watch the sunset, I'd gladly follow you."

"You mean that?" he asked, his half-smile revealing his gap and a faint dimple.

"Absolutely. My tastes. . .are changing, as it were. I'm truly grateful to be out with you tonight, wherever we go."

"Well, I definitely can't shirk this one now that I'm a manager." He sank into his seat, defeated. "Maybe we can enjoy the dinner, dance a few numbers, and then head out."

"Sounds great." Anywhere with Levi sounded wonderful.

As their carriage waited in line to drop them off at the front of the Yesler mansion, he reached toward her, grabbing her gloved hand. Her heart soared and she swallowed hard.

"Thank you for coming," he said earnestly. "It's an honor to bring the most beautiful girl in Seattle to dinner and introduce her to the people I work with. Plus, we can chat about everyone's odd fashion choices. And I'd love to have your advice about a couple work issues I've been having."

She beamed, feeling heat on her cheeks. Levi winked at her in that way he always had, teasing but meaningful, and he jumped out of the carriage as it came to a stop at the entrance. He held his hand up to her and assumed the disinterested face of a hired coachman, though the corners of his mouth quirked up as if he was trying not to smile.

With her hand in his, she seemed to float to the ground. Once inside, the electric buzz of the house surrounded them. She clung to Levi's arm and he squeezed back. She felt safe for the first time in months, maybe years.

Soon she was introduced to a slew of people. They were men and women she'd never seen in Seattle society, but they were all quite sophisticated. The Yesler circle was certainly something she'd never seen the inside of before.

One lady with dark brown hair looked around her age. When she was introduced to her, Emily felt a rush of excitement.

"This is Isabelle Greene," Levi said, gesturing toward the lady. "Please meet the lovely Emily Watson."

She blushed and put her hand out. Isabelle grinned warmly and shook her hand.

"Pleasure to meet you, Emily. Will you both sit by my husband and I? I'd love to hear all about you."

The feeling in Emily's chest was somewhere between elation and nerves. It all felt too good to be true.

As they sat for the meal—roasted wild turkey with cornbread stuffing—she admired the glass chandelier and large white pillars that stood on either side of the dining room entrance. The crystal wine glasses sparkled as they were filled with red wine by the hired help—women in muted colors.

Isabelle pointed toward a short man with graying hair who stood on the opposite end of the table. "I do believe Mr. Wright is about to regale us with a speech."

And just as she finished saying the words, the man raised his crystal glass in the air and a hush came over the large room. Emily smiled at her new friend as they exchanged an amused glance.

"Ladies and gentlemen, if I could have your attention please. I'd like to make a short speech in Henry's honor." He nodded to Yesler who sat beside him, eyes twinkling.

"Forty years ago, this man threw his boiler off the ship to float ashore and put his engine on a raft."

A soft laugh and a few gasps sounded from the table.

"He reassembled his mill in record time and started producing the lumber that would allow the first newcomers to Seattle to replace their log cabins with proper frame houses of excellent quality. Sometimes that first mill was run twenty-four hours per day to keep up with demand in split shifts. Not only that, but did you younger folks know that Henry himself invented the first water system this city had?"

A few voices murmured to each other, but no one responded.

"Well, his Seattle Water Company drew water from a spring by Third Street and used hollow logs to bring it on into town."

Emily leaned in to whisper to Levi, "I sure appreciate our running water. I had no idea that Yesler started it all here."

He smiled and put a hand over hers on the table, and she drew in a sharp breath at the touch.

The short gentleman cleared his throat and went on. "A few decades and a couple lumber mills later, he became our mayor and served two terms with his lovely wife, Sarah, by his side, God rest her soul."

The nods and words of agreement that sounded around the table told Emily that Sarah was beloved by all.

"And even now as he plans to step away from the everyday operations, this man is still employing most of the able-bodied men around here. Please raise your glass to our very own Henry Yesler!"

A cheer sounded nearly in unison as every person in the room lifted their wine glasses and clinked them with one another, mumbling words of appreciation for the host.

The honor bestowed made Emily feel grateful to be part of such a close group. It was clear that he treated his men well.

After the meal, they excused themselves and found a spot around the dance floor that had been created in the expansive parlor. A large mahogany grandfather clock stood at one end of the room, which reminded her of the one she'd had in her former home with her late husband.

But those memories seemed distant, nearly a lifetime ago. Now, the energy buzzed through her simply being in Levi's presence, being able to look into his eyes, and him being able to nearly read her mind. It was all so intimate, and she wouldn't have traded it for anything.

The quartet began playing "The Blue Danube Waltz" and Levi lifted an eyebrow, offering his hand. She took it, and he lifted it up for her to do a slow spin before whisking her onto the dance floor.

When had he learned to dance like that? It was as if he was still her childhood best friend on the inside but had become some debonair gentleman on the outside. Handsome, sure of himself, but with the same green eyes that could see inside her soul.

As the waltz ended nearly ten minutes later, he dipped her seductively and froze, staring into her eyes. She fought the urge to look around her, curious to see if others thought this was inappropriate, but instead she fixed her eyes on his and soaked up the clear love in his gaze.

"You trust me, right?" he asked, so sure of himself that she wanted to tease him.

Instead, she nodded, and he pulled her up slowly and into an embrace, kissing her forehead. Emily shut her eyes tight, shutting out the gazes and the world around her. Who cared what these people thought? She was home.

"How are you doing?" he whispered. "I know this must be a lot for you after. . ."

She smiled timidly, somewhat uncomfortable having a light shined on her time of grieving. "Perhaps one more dance and then we excuse ourselves?"

"As you wish." He twirled her once more as the quartet began a spirited number.

They moved as one across the dance floor, looking as much at each other as possible without bumping into their fellow dancers.

When the song finished, Levi grabbed her hand and they made their way back to the main entrance of the house. She waved good-bye to Isabelle and her husband, who were still spinning on the dance floor, and her friend waved back merrily. Hopefully, she could get her address from Levi and perhaps call on her soon.

Mr. Yesler stood near the door wishing couples farewell as they put on hats and coats.

When it was their turn, Emily smiled broadly. She'd heard much about Henry Yesler, and it was truly an honor to meet him.

As Mr. Yesler shook Levi's hand and asked him about his month at the mill, she stood quietly beside him until he looked over to her, as she had learned to do.

"What a delight to meet you and have you for a guest in my home," the older man said.

"Thank you for having us." She curtsied without thinking, not sure if that was appropriate.

He nodded graciously, and they were out the door, entering yet another hired carriage.

Once inside, she blew out a relieved sigh. Those kinds of events used to exhilarate her, but now she only wanted to be alone with Levi. It was pleasant simply to talk with him about life, or anything.

He leaned forward, taking off his hat and sweeping his light brown hair back. The color in his cheeks made him look youthful, but the sharp angle of his stubbly jaw said otherwise. He held out both of his hands to her.

She leaned forward toward him, putting her hands into his. His were warm. Hers were cold. Their faces were inches apart when the horses lurched forward and they nearly knocked heads together.

Levi laughed. "There's no one else I'd rather knock heads against in a choppy carriage ride."

Emily laughed too, but then his eyes turned serious and he leaned closer. With the way the carriage swayed, he was at times inches from her face and other times farther as they hit minor bumps along the cobblestone street.

Each time his face came closer, her heart squeezed and she wondered if he would kiss her.

And then he did. The only places they touched were their hands and lips. In order to maintain the kiss, he put a great deal of force into it, otherwise the carriage would sway them apart. Emily's pulse shot through her like lightning in her veins. His lips pressed softly against hers despite the force with which he kept them there.

Then the carriage lurched once more and the connection broke.

Levi blushed and squeezed her hands. "I suppose that's a sign I'm moving too quickly."

A self-conscious warmth covered her cheeks, and she bit her bottom lip. It still tingled from his touch.

"I like being with you." He let go of her hands and rested his back against his seat.

"Likewise." She leaned back but not against the seat. She pulled her spine upright as she hadn't done in months, and it felt good. It felt like herself. "That was quite the party. I had no idea you were such an important man."

He laughed. "So I might persuade you to join me for another evening out sometime?"

"I think you might," she said with a smile.

CHAPTER TWENTY
THE SUSPECT

Anna | July 1891

By the end of July, Anna felt confident in her strength and the training she and Ben had completed together.

Without having to hide her training at home this time, the two of them spent most evenings following each other up and down the stairs with backpacks full of books. After her first climb, she knew the descent was just as important to train for. And all the while, the puppy bounded up and down after them.

At first, it proved breathless work, but after it had become a habit, they had both gotten more fit. Lately, they'd been having extensive conversations on their staircase treks.

Balance was something that had been a challenge for her before, so she did many of her mundane household tasks on one foot or the other. Even at the bookstore while she worked, anytime she needed to stand in one place for a few minutes, she would become a flamingo.

On a Sunday afternoon, a few days before they planned to take the train south to Yelm to join the team, Anna and Ben spent the day at the Gallagher house. They arrived midday, bringing Comma with them. She bounded along on her leash, sniffing every flower on the walk over.

Anna looked forward to a few hours of chatting with her family and then helping Greta prepare the dinner, like old times.

Once they arrived, Ben tied the leash to the front porch and ruffled the fur around Comma's collar.

"Greta doesn't want you making a mess of her house, so you'll have to stay out here. Catch some flies for us, all right?"

The puppy seemed to understand her objective and began to sniff along the side of the house.

"Couldn't we take her off the leash so she can roam farther?" Anna asked, feeling badly for the sweet pup.

"She's not familiar with the woods around here. I'm afraid she might wander off too far and we'd have to spend all evening looking for her."

She nodded sadly and then bent down to kiss the puppy's soft fur before they went inside.

Her grandfather and Greta sat in front of the fire, and so they joined them. After the initial good mornings, they all fell into a peaceful silence while looking at the fire.

Then Ben turned to the older man and asked, "What was Anna like as a young girl?"

She blushed, and all eyes turned to her grandfather.

"Well, she's always been free-spirited, but she did become awfully quiet after my son and Mollie died. And although she and I had always been close, I had no idea how to raise a young lady, especially one as stubborn as her mother."

"And he'd recently lost his own wife as well," Greta added

thoughtfully. She reached out and put a hand on his knee. It was a sorrow they were both familiar with.

"She'd have known how to love the kids well," he went on. "But after such a heavy loss, we needed a fresh start."

"I know Ben and I are both very grateful you made that choice," Greta said, winking at Ben.

"Absolutely," he said with a grin.

"And when we moved out here, Anna helped me grow the finest Black English currants to make our own wine," he said. "Coincidentally, they're the only English thing on earth which I approve."

He roared with laughter, and Greta shook her head.

"And he sure enjoys his wine to the fullest," she added.

"Now, now," he said, canting his head to the side. "I've changed my ways a bit, haven't I? Since last summer when this lassie took off with no warning, leaving me to drink myself silly."

"Don't go blamin' your granddaughter for your own choices," Greta scolded, then she smiled. "But yes, dear, you've come an awfully long way since then, and I'm proud of ya."

Her grandfather beamed and stared into the fire.

When a knock sounded at the door, Anna locked eyes with Greta. Not many neighbors came calling on a Sunday, and they weren't expecting anyone.

Greta stood to greet the new arrivals. "Well, if it isn't the other Mr. and Mrs. Chambers!"

Anna saw Ben stiffen and toss her a surprised glance. He stood swiftly and strode toward the door.

"To what do we owe the pleasure of this surprise visit, Mother?" he asked her as he gave her a tentative hug.

"Well, we knew you two were going to head up the mountain at the start of August, so we wanted to make sure we came up to visit before you left. To tell you good luck. Isn't that right, honey?"

"Right, yes," Dr. Chambers echoed. "The University in Berkeley is out for the summer, and we'd planned to travel anyway. Why not come up north to visit our mountaineering son?"

"And daughter!" Greta added merrily. "Anna is quite the mountaineer herself."

Anna felt herself blush, and she greeted her in-laws warmly.

"I hope you'll stay for dinner," she said hopefully.

Or maybe she hoped they'd say no. Her feelings were torn, and she still got a strange feeling around Ben's father. Something didn't seem quite right with him.

"How about we take you to that play we talked about at your wedding?" Beth asked. "I'm sorry we had to leave so suddenly after the wedding, but your father wasn't feeling his best and wanted to get on the road."

"Well, tonight we're having dinner with Oscar and Greta, but you're welcome to join us," Ben answered without a hint of regret. "Perhaps we can look into the theater for tomorrow night."

"That would be fine, darling," his mother said, kissing his cheek. "It's a pleasure to see you. We'd love to stay for dinner, wouldn't we, dear?"

"Yes, quite right," Dr. Chambers mumbled.

Greta got right to work in the kitchen, and Anna stole away to help her.

"How odd for them to arrive unexpectedly, don't you think?" she asked as she donned her apron from its hook.

"If you and Ben moved away, we'd come and visit you any chance we got." Greta put a fork into the kettle to test the potatoes. "They're done."

"But wouldn't you send word first?" she asked quietly, glancing toward the living room. "What if we hadn't been in town?"

Greta replied quickly. "But you are, and now we all get to have a lovely meal together. I think it's wonderful."

Anna knew she was attempting to smooth over the uncomfortable social situation for propriety's sake.

While Greta drained the water out of the kettle, Anna poured milk into a saucepan until it hit the boiling point and then added butter. When the potatoes were good and smashed back in the drained kettle, she carefully poured about half of her mixture in. Greta began whipping them with her slotted spoon and nodded toward the kitchen.

"Why don't you go out there and offer wine?"

Anna sighed and poked her head out of the kitchen. Ben looked a little uneasy, so she moved toward them.

"Can I offer you all any wine?" she asked.

Ben nodded and sent her an unreadable expression, then chewed his lip.

She returned a few minutes later with a bottle and began pouring for each of them.

"Have preparations been made for your trip, dear?" Ben's mother asked.

"Everything we can do in advance is mostly taken care of." Anna sat and took a small sip of her wine. "Honestly, it comes down to loads of walking for days, and then a day or more of intense climbing in snow and ice. Then the whole thing in reverse."

Dr. Chambers's mouth dropped open slightly. "You don't ride a horse or take a carriage as far as possible?"

Ben cleared his throat. "We take the train as far as Yelm, but from there we mostly walk."

"We do have pack animals, but they carry our stuff," she added. It made perfect sense to her, but judging by the look on his face, Ben's father still seemed confused. What more did he want?

Greta arrived with roasted chicken, and her grandfather stood to help her bring in the other serving dishes with the mashed potatoes and roasted carrots.

"And what do you wear for these excursions?" Dr. Chambers asked, his voice wry.

Ben raised his eyebrows and shrugged. "We don't need to wear coats and scarves until we gain elevation."

Anna swallowed uncomfortably. That question was definitely targeted directly at her. "Last year, I wore men's trousers after arriving in Yelm. We have to cross through a large river, and it makes that more convenient. Also, with the ice and snow, it wouldn't be sensible to wear a dress."

"I should think that it's always sensible for a woman to wear women's clothes." Dr. Chambers said this without looking at her. Rather, he folded his napkin and then placed it on his lap in what seemed to her like a grand show of propriety.

Her stomach churned at his words, and she longed to defend herself but didn't want to sound as if his comments had hurt her.

"That may be so in town or at certain events, but in the mountains, I'm sure it's a different story," Greta piped in.

"Other women explorers I've read about have chosen different options, but I quite liked the pants I wore last year and plan to bring them along again." She took a bite and smiled coolly at her father-in-law, who all but rolled his eyes with his clear disapproval.

"Isabella Bird climbed all over the Rocky Mountains in fascinating clothing." Anna stood suddenly, excited that she remembered, and began walking toward the front door to find her bag.

"Oh, don't worry, she's brought the book with her," Ben said with an amused expression.

She returned with her copy of *A Lady's Life in the Rocky Mountains*.

"Do tell us about it," Beth said, looking to her husband in what Anna thought was delight. It was odd that she didn't seem to sense his discomfort about the subject.

"I'll read a passage in which she describes her dress."

For the benefit of other lady travelers, I wish to explain that my "Hawaiian riding dress" is the "American Lady's Mountain Dress," a half-fitting jacket, a skirt reaching to the ankles, and full Turkish trousers gathered into frills falling over the boots—a thoroughly serviceable and feminine costume for mountaineering and other rough traveling, as in the Alps or any other part of the world.

"That seems like a lot of fabric to haul around for the warmer parts of the hike," Ben said.

"But at least it's proper attire for a lady," Dr. Chambers said stiffly.

"Is there something you want to say, Father?" Ben asked, tilting his head in a look of challenge.

Dr. Chambers lifted both hands in a defensive way. "I'm simply making a point. I'm all for women being part of society in a constructive way. I have no doubt that women are every bit as intelligent as men. However, it does their kind no favors when women act unladylike or take it upon themselves to behave exactly like a man."

Ben's chest puffed out as if he were about to yell, but her grandfather beat him to it.

"I won't have you coming into my house and insulting my granddaughter," he said, voice booming. His face was darkening to a shade of pink she knew all too well.

"No, it's fine," she said as quickly as she could. "I welcome a differing opinion, and I'm happy to discuss it."

Dr. Chambers nodded graciously to her. "Thank you, dear. You are certainly well-bred and otherwise quite sensible. Now, might you consider wearing something more appropriate on this climb?"

"That's enough!" Ben's voice rang loud in the small dining room as he stood. "We're going to summit a mountain. It's an incredible feat, and all you want to talk about is fashion and propriety. What kind of intellectual are you?"

He reached for Anna's hand, pulling her to stand, and she had never loved him more. "I'd ask you to leave, but this isn't my home."

"Well, I'll gladly do it," her grandfather said, crossing his arms.

"No, let us go," Anna said. The commotion was upsetting, but with both her grandfather and Ben having her back, she'd never felt more supported.

Ben's mother looked as if she were about to cry, which made Anna feel sorry for her. She didn't seem to see how much her husband despised what they were doing.

Anna quickly donned her shawl and put her shoes on while the silence in the dining room sat like thick butter.

Not a single word more was said as they both walked out the door to gather the puppy and head home.

THE NEXT MORNING, Anna woke to a frantic banging on the front door of their house. She opened her eyes slowly and saw the sun had only just risen. It couldn't be later than five.

Ben was already putting on his pants and rushing out their bedroom door, shirt in hand.

She sat up, putting her feet on the cool wood floor, then stood to grab something presentable—her yellow calico dress that was slung over the chair near her bed, ready for mending. It was only a ripped shoulder seam and would work fine for an emergency.

On her way down the stairs, the front door shut and she heard a horse gallop away.

"What's happened?" she asked. "Who was that?"

Ben's face was white and he inhaled sharply. "Emily's father. The bookstore. . . There was a fire."

"What?" She froze in place on the stairs. Memories of the great fire the year before flooded her mind. "Grandfather wasn't there, was he?"

"No, Mr. Taylor believes it started a few hours ago," he replied, walking up the stairs toward her. "The fire department got there quickly and put the flames out—none of the surrounding buildings were affected."

"How could a fire have started in the middle of the night when no one was there?"

"He said they're looking into it now, searching the premises and trying to interview the other shop owners and people who were around this morning."

Perhaps her grandfather had left a candle burning? She didn't even want to say it out loud. He was getting old, but he wasn't all that forgetful. Since she and Ben were preparing to leave on their trip the next day, he had already hired another person to help him, but she wouldn't start until Monday.

"We should go down there at once," she said, her arms crossed over her chest.

Ben hurried back down the stairs.

She supposed they should also stop by the hotel where his parents were staying to let them know what happened. They wouldn't be able to go to the theater with them after all. They had much to do before leaving south on the train, and now things had gotten even more complicated.

By the time they reached the bookstore, the fire hoses had been wrapped up and loaded. A few police officers lingered around the scene, including Mr. Taylor making notes in a small book in his hand.

The charred wood of the front door put a devastating lump in Anna's throat. Singed leather book spines lay in heaps and piles, their pages burnt to ashes.

She found Greta and gave her a long hug. The older woman's eyes were bloodshot.

"I don't know who would've done such a thing. And after making it through the fire last year, it's just horrible."

"Surely, it was some kind of accident," Anna told her soothingly.

"You didn't hear? Mr. Taylor is sure of it now. Arson."

She stepped back and looked over at Ben, who was talking with her grandfather.

Who could harbor that much hate against them? And was it the same person who had been vandalizing the bookstore before and leaving threatening notes?

Without meaning to, her mind focused on Ben's father. She had never brought up her fear with Ben, but it had lingered in her heart. The last time the store was attacked had been the night after his parents had arrived, and after Dr. Chambers had menacingly spoken to her about knowing her place. And now the bookstore had been completely destroyed right after their arrival. It was uncanny.

But apparently she didn't need to say anything about it to Ben. His eyes were lit with fire.

He came up behind her and whispered in her ear, "I'll be back."

"Where are you going?" she called after him.

"The hotel."

She chased after him, her boots pounding the wood-planked sidewalk.

When they arrived at the Occidental Hotel, he asked the gentleman in the lobby which room his parents were in. Then he ran up the stairs to the second floor, barely giving Anna a chance to catch up as she flew behind him holding her skirts so she wouldn't land on her face.

He knocked on their door, and his mother came at once.

"Good morning, Ben. I'll come out and join you. Your father was out late last night at the tavern, and he has an awful headache. He doesn't want to be disturbed."

He put his foot in the door. "I need to speak with him right now."

Her eyes widened. "Not now, dear—"

But he'd already opened the door wide. Anna wasn't sure if she should follow him in, so she stayed in the hallway with his mother. Dr. Chambers was sitting in a dressing gown on a chair near the window, his head in his hands.

"It was you, wasn't it?" Ben accused.

Anna swallowed hard, biting her lip. He'd come to this conclusion on his own, and she was glad of it, but she was also grateful she hadn't had to convince him of it.

"What are you talking about?" Dr. Chambers growled, clearly alarmed by the entry but not moving to stand.

"You said she shouldn't climb the mountain. You've kept saying it. And every time you come to town, something happens to the Gallagher bookstore."

"I don't know what you're talking about, son," he said quietly. "But you're talking way too loud for this early in the morning. And yes, I certainly do think your wife should not be a mountaineer. I can't be the only one."

"Do you deny that you burnt their bookstore to the ground?" Ben asked.

His mother gasped.

Dr. Chambers waved his hand dismissively. "I won't even respond to that."

Ben stood for a moment, perhaps thinking of what to say next, then he turned quickly and walked back out the door.

"Mother, I don't want to see him again." He hesitated in front of his mother, apparently deciding whether or not he should say anything more.

With a quick kiss on his mother's cheek, he grabbed Anna's hand and took off down the hallway toward the stairs.

CHAPTER TWENTY-ONE
FOR THE LIGHTS THAT SHINE

ANNA | AUGUST 1891

Before the sun rose on the morning of their departure, Anna stared up at the ceiling of their bedroom. Ben's dramatic confrontation with his dad had been intense, but she was grateful he was on her side. How could Dr. Chambers be so cruel? And what exactly was the point of destroying the bookstore? It wasn't as if that would stop her from summiting, and it certainly hadn't put her in any immediate danger.

Perhaps he'd hoped that the devastation, and how upset her family was, would cause her to stay back—to "stay in her place." It was too infuriating. Other times when the store had been vandalized, or when people had stopped by to make their opinions known, it had been more about boycotting their business on account of her lifestyle choices. At no point had she believed it would escalate to complete destruction.

In the dark, she envisioned the snow-capped peaks, the shimmering glaciers, and the assortment of mountain wildflowers. It was impossible to sleep, especially knowing how early they needed to rise to catch their train.

What a different experience from a year ago. Now she was happily married, she didn't have to sneak out of the house, and she didn't need to fret about whether her family or Ben would accept her mountaineering secret.

She did need to worry about an even further strained relationship between Ben and his father though, and the complete destruction of the family bookstore. Every sane person in Seattle had purchased fire insurance after the debacle of the Great Fire of 1889. So the loss wasn't felt as hard as it might have been. And Ben had already offered to cover all the expenses that their fire insurance didn't cover. Still, it was alarming to have your family business destroyed because of hate. Essentially, it was her fault. If she weren't pushing the boundaries of acceptable behavior, none of it would have happened.

Perhaps it was a bad omen, a sign they would be injured, or worse, on the mountain. Her mind spun out of control as the sun began to lighten the horizon before it rose. She shuddered and slipped quietly out of the bed so as not to wake Ben.

Greta and her grandfather had come over the night before, after they'd left the remains of the bookstore. It had been good to see them one last time before their trip.

And before they'd left, Greta had offered to braid Anna's hair in preparation for the journey in a special double braid she'd learned in Sweden. Anna reached up and ran her fingers gently along the side of one braid to where it joined the other near the nape of her neck. It was a special moment they had shared, especially since she hadn't helped with her hair since the wedding. If she was careful, her hair might stay exactly as it was for nearly the whole two weeks they would be away.

Downstairs, she looked over the bags they had packed the night before. Their equipment was the best that could be purchased in Seattle—there had been no need to order anything from a catalogue. They had bought her climbing boots months ago, and she'd been hiking in them for so long now that they fit perfectly and were entirely broken in. There would be no unneeded blisters or injuries because of carelessness this time.

The journal Ben had given her was tucked neatly next to her clothing, and the memory of the proposal wrapped a cloak of reassurance around her.

A light tapping came from the door, and she looked out the window in the early morning light to make sure it wasn't one of Ben's parents. Would she let them in if it had been one of them?

But it was Heather, and Anna was overjoyed to see her.

"We were going to bring Comma by your house on the way," she said, waving her in.

"Michael told me about the bookstore. I was horrified to hear the news."

"Yes, it's awful. I'll make coffee and we can chat." Anna sighed deeply. "It's such a wonderful surprise for you to come over."

As she put the water on to boil, she recounted the events of the fire and the subsequent confrontation between Ben and his father.

"It certainly sounds like he's to blame," Heather offered. "It's good Ben sees that, but it must also be difficult for him."

"I know," Anna replied, frowning. "That's exactly it. I'm glad I didn't have to point out the obvious to him, but I'm also sad he has to deal with this. It's a lot of pressure and guilt he's putting on himself when I'm the real reason for the hate."

"Some people have hatred in their hearts, Anna." Heather sipped her coffee slowly. "Maybe one day Ben's father will change, as your grandfather did."

She was at first taken aback that Heather had compared Ben's father with her own loving grandfather, but her friend was right. Hating someone because of the tribe they were born into, and hating someone because of what they chose to do in their life—it was all evil.

"How have you been?" she asked, setting her mug down. "How is life in the city with Michael?"

"You know I wasn't thrilled about moving here," Heather said, shifting in her seat. "I feel I don't belong—"

"Well, I often feel I barely belong, and I grew up here!" she exclaimed.

Heather was quiet for a moment. "Yes, but that's different, much different."

"You're right. I'm sorry." She sighed, trying to think of another way to empathize with her friend but came up short.

"I have made a Duwamish friend though," Heather said with a smile. "She sells baskets at the fruit market, like my family makes. Do you remember watching them weave at salmon fishing last year?"

"I do. It was beautiful. I'm sorry I couldn't join you all this year."

Heather nodded with a smile. "Michael seems to be doing better, actually, in his mind, having Pisha and me with him. His spirits seem high."

"That's wonderful. I'm glad to hear that."

"I visited my grandmother out at the cabin yesterday," Heather said, looking down at her hands. "I miss her dearly."

"I do know how that feels," Anna said, the same sorrow in her own chest. "I still miss my parents, but doing what I love makes me feel closer to them."

"Like climbing the mountain," Heather said, smiling.

"Exactly."

"I was able to salvage some of the herbs from her garden. I brought them to our house here and planted them in the garden that Michael tilled. He bought the lot behind our house, so we have lots of grassy hills for Pisha to play on. And Comma, for the time being. Michael said he may even build a barn next summer. I'd love to have a horse and maybe some chickens." Heather grinned.

Anna was delighted to hear the tone in her friend's voice as she described her new situation. "I'm glad for you. It all sounds wonderful. And your grandmother would love to know that part of her is with you always."

She stood, gathering her skirts. "I'll be right back with bread and cheese."

Heather stood as well. "No, you need to prepare your things. I'll make breakfast for you and Ben while you get ready."

Anna hugged her. "You're such a dear friend."

"Well, I'm happy to have you close by now. One of the few benefits of living in this city I don't love." Heather offered a half-smile, then shrugged, heading inside the house.

In the living room, Ben was moving around checking their equipment, hair tousled from sleep. Comma circled around his feet with a concerned expression. When might he stop looking so handsome to her? She hoped it wouldn't be any time soon.

"Good morning, Heather," he said. "We sincerely appreciate your willingness to watch this fur ball."

"I'm happy to help in any way I can," she replied. "About to make flapjacks."

"Sounds wonderful. Thank you," he said, stretching his arms up to the ceiling.

While Heather moved into the kitchen, Anna gathered up the few things she'd send with Comma. She already had a favorite rug to sleep on, so she rolled it up tightly and set it next to her tin water dish. The rope that hung next to the front door served as her leash, and Anna collected that too.

Seemingly uncomfortable with these odd movements, Comma whined and nuzzled her ankles. It tugged at her heart, and she bent down to pick the ball of fluff into her arms. The little thing had solidly nestled a place into her heart, and she'd miss her terribly while they were gone.

"It'll only be a few days," she whispered before attaching the rope to her blue collar.

Ben came over and kissed the puppy on her head, then ruffled her soft ears. "She'll do great with Heather. Pisha will have a grand old time too."

Heather started lacing her boots as soon as the feast was ready and placed on the table. She'd also packed extra provisions for lunch and dinner for their travels that day. Anna walked her out the door, Comma in tow, and then hugged her friend one last time.

"Once again, you will be great," Heather said with a nod. "No matter the outcome, you will have a good experience and get to share that with the one you love. All while feeling closer to your parents."

Anna looked down at her feet and crossed her arms over her chest. "The way you say that makes me feel like we won't summit."

Heather laughed. "No. I think you will have luck with the weather. I wish you all the best."

Anna watched her walk away with Comma at her heels as the summer sun began to rise. The puppy looked back at her continually, which made her sad, so she turned away and back to the task at hand. They didn't need to be at the train station for another hour and a half, but they had much left to do and a lot of equipment to get there.

Inside the house, Ben was sitting down at the breakfast table.

"We should eat as much as we can," he said, patting his stomach. "And luckily for us, this smells delicious."

She joined him at the table, squeezing his hand. "I'm much less nervous this time around, but I still feel uneasy. There's a multitude of unknowns ahead of us."

"We'll face them together," he said, bringing a forkful to his mouth and then leaning back into his chair comfortably.

"It feels that if I don't summit this time, I shouldn't bother trying again," she said, putting a small bite into her mouth.

"You're thinking about it too much. Isn't the beauty in the climb, and the experience of preparing and getting there? Even at basecamp, the views will be more stunning than anything I've ever seen. And what was the part in John Muir's account you shared with me last night? About lofty mountain tops…"

She smiled, and a gentle peace settled in her chest. "You're right. I've memorized it to hold in my mind. *More pleasure is to be found at the foot of the mountains than on their tops. Doubly happy, however, is the man to whom lofty mountain tops are within reach, for the lights that shine there illumine all that lies below.*"

The lights—had she missed them last time? Or maybe they

could only be seen from the peak. What light did he speak of, and what exactly would be illuminated?

With more questions than answers, she finished her breakfast and laced her boots. Her goggles, crampons, and alpenstock were packed together with their tent and provisions. She had one change of clothes—pants—along with the fur vest Heather had made for her last year.

They'd planned to walk to the train station rather than taking a coach or a streetcar. Ben reached for her hand as they stepped onto the street.

The sky was filled with a faint bluish-purple haze, which lightened as they got closer to the station. They didn't chat on their walk like they usually did. A heavy excitement buoyed her, and something about the silence made the moment special.

The train ride was loud and rocky, but she managed to fall asleep for a few minutes here and there. The views were fantastic though, and she hated missing them. Rolling hills covered in tall grass were interspersed between both large and small rivers. The Puget Sound was on the right-hand side of the train, but it wasn't always visible. By the time they reached Yelm, her excitement had come to a crescendo, and she squeezed Ben's hand tightly.

At the station, Mr. Flannaghan waited for them—black suit, top hat, and all. Her mind flashed back to a year prior when she had been nervous to meet him, and she relaxed knowing she could entrust her life to him now.

"It's a pleasure to finally meet you, Mr. Chambers," Mr. Flannaghan said, shaking Ben's hand heartily.

"I have to thank you kindly, Mr. Flannaghan, for taking such good care of Anna last year," Ben said. "She said she was in good hands with you and the team, and I believe her."

"It was a delight to have her with us, and even more so to have her return this year. And for you to join us too, of course." His dark green eyes danced. "We're camped out in the fields tonight and a couple fellows are holed up in a barn. Let's go."

As Mr. Flannaghan spun on his heel and briskly walked off the train station platform, Ben turned to her with a grin. "After you."

At the camp, John sat near the fire hunched over his notebook. He looked up as they drew near.

"Well, if it isn't Anna!" he said, closing his notebook and rising to stand. "You must be her husband. Pleasure to meet you, sir."

Ben took John's outstretched hand and shook it. "Nice to meet you, John. We were quite pleased to read the article you wrote last year about Anna on the mountain."

Anna smiled but wondered if he might write another one about this ascent. How much backlash might she and her family receive? Yet the bookstore was already burned to the ground, she thought cynically.

"John, I'm delighted to see you again. It's nice to have the old team back together."

"It sure is. Lou and Peter are 'round about here somewhere." He sat back down, pushing his glasses up his nose.

Anna looked around for a good spot to set up their tent. They found a reasonable place near the fire and close to John's tent.

As she and Ben began to make camp, Lou came whistling around a nearby barn, then stopped short when he saw them. Anna held her breath, wondering how he might receive her this time. He had seemed almost proud of her after last year's summit attempt, but who knew whether he was glad to have her back.

"Well, well." He sauntered closer, spitting tobacco into the tall grass. "Anna done got herself a man."

Ben lifted his eyebrows, glancing at her. Then he tipped his hat at Lou. "I'm Ben Chambers. Anna tells me you are quite the accomplished mountaineer, Lou."

"She ain't lyin' about that." Lou puffed out his chest and almost smiled. "I expect you've found suitable boots this time?"

Her cheeks warmed. "That I have. And I've been hiking and training in them for months."

"Atta girl," he said, folding his arms and staring off toward the mountain. "Ben, do you have much experience with mountains?"

"No, sir, but I'm thrilled to learn," he said, stepping beside Lou to look up at the peak.

"I think we have as good a shot as last year. I expect to summit once again. This'll be my fourth time if we succeed, and I hope the whole team can make it this time." With that, he walked toward the fire and sat across from John without another word.

Anna smiled at Ben and shrugged. After they had finished with the tent, she showed him the ponies and two mules that would be with them until base camp. The animals seemed bored, grazing in the grass and occasionally looking up at them sleepily.

When Peter stepped up behind them, she turned to greet him. His light blond hair shone in the sunlight, and he folded his arms over his barrel chest.

"I'm Peter." He lifted his head high. "You're the one who let a woman sneak away last year to join our little group."

Peter smirked at Ben, which reminded Anna starkly of the fact that he was the one who had gotten drunk and attempted to open her tent last year. It was something she hadn't mentioned to Ben. Nothing had happened, and she had been safe after all. Even if she'd clutched her knife and barely slept at all that night.

Ben lifted his eyebrows slightly and cocked his head to the side. They were both about the same height and build.

"I hope you don't mind that I've come to join her this year," he said with an amused smile and a hint of a challenge.

Peter rolled his eyes and walked away.

After he was some distance away, Ben grabbed her hand. "You didn't tell me you had such charming company last year."

She laughed and shook her head.

After a quick dinner by the fire, everyone pulled out their bills and handed them to Mr. Flannaghan for their share of the provisions and use of the pack animals. He folded them neatly and put them in his suit jacket pocket.

"We'll start early tomorrow, so let's make it an early night."

Anna and Ben were the last ones remaining at the fire before turning in. A small sliver of moon was rising on the horizon, and two stars had joined it in the slate blue sky.

"You're going to be great," he whispered in her ear.

CHAPTER TWENTY-TWO

A FAMILIAR FEAR

EMILY

E mily hurried to finish her morning work on the farm so she could have some leisure time that afternoon. Months ago, time alone with nothing particular to do would have made her melancholy, but now that she was in love and had already paid nearly seventy dollars of her late husband's debts, she relished a sunny day full of possibilities. She'd also received an invitation from her new friend Isabelle to join her for tea the following Tuesday. Life was starting to feel truly wonderful again.

Levi had a meeting at the mill and then an inspection, so she expected he would be busy most of the day, but she knew he would likely stop by in the evening to wish her goodnight as he usually did.

She decided to make a pie for him, and she left for town to get fresh cherries. The sky was clear blue and the heat of the summer morning warmed her back as she strode into town.

There was a little old lady sitting at the edge of the market surrounded by empty baskets, and Emily wandered over to her. The lady was Duwamish like Heather, and she noticed the beautiful geometric patterns on the baskets.

"How much?" she asked.

"Ten cents, miss," the Duwamish woman replied.

Emily picked out a medium-sized basket with orange squares and blue triangles.

"It's lovely." She smiled kindly at the woman, handed her the coins, then rounded the corner back to the market where the fruit stands gleamed with colors.

Filling her basket with bright red cherries delighted her and reminded her of picking cherries in the Gallagher tree with Levi years ago.

In the busy street market, she blushed from the memory. She wanted to run to Levi right now and kiss him just because she could. Instead, she'd let him do his important work, the work that would allow them to have a life together. And she'd happily make him a cherry pie, wondering how often he thought of that special memory.

Once at home, she got to work right away. She remembered fondly the new-fangled refrigerator that she'd just received in her old house with Charles. It seemed like something from the future compared to the ice box they'd had before. And it was a true luxury compared with what they had in her father's home—no ice. It would have been much easier to make the pie crust with a way to keep the dough ball cool while she made the cherry filling. But putting it in a bowl in a pan of cold water would do fine, as it always had.

Serenely, she mixed the flour and salt, then spooned the lard in to blend with her fingers. Pitting the cherries was calming, and she did her work all while daydreaming. With a flourish of her wrist, she dusted the wooden table with flour and placed the ball of dough upon it. She rolled it flat, moving from the center outward in each direction. She used her mother's tin leaf press to make a wreath of crust around the top.

After putting the pie in the oven, she sat on the porch, enjoying the summer breeze in her hair. Bees buzzed around the daisies in the grass below her, and the shade of the porch provided relief.

In the distance, a figure walked toward the house. It moved slowly, and the shoulders were slumped. It took her a few minutes to realize it was Levi.

She stood and started walking to meet him. It looked like something was wrong, and she picked up her pace. So much of her happiness lately depended on him being her constant, and the thought of him changing his mind about her or being angry with her about something made her stomach drop.

When she finally met up with him, he reached out and embraced her, resting his head on her shoulder.

"It was my fault. I was in charge."

"What happened? What was your fault?" she asked, afraid of the answer.

Levi didn't let go of her. "One of my men. He died today at the mill. An accident, but it's my fault."

She squeezed him tighter and then turned toward the house and began to lead him to it.

Once inside, he spilled everything, going into detail over the gruesome death that had happened at his workplace.

"I'm going to put in my resignation tomorrow," he said, eyes bloodshot.

She didn't know exactly what that meant for him, or what it would mean for their courtship.

"I can catch another fishing boat heading up north for the season. It's nearly over, but at least I could pick up some work that way." He wiped a tear away before it fell. "What if they press charges against me?"

Finally, she realized the implications. Levi could be jobless, without a career and with no stability.

"I understand if this changes your feelings for me," he said, clearing his throat.

She stood. "I'll be right back."

She entered the kitchen, her mind spinning. The pie was nearly done, and the sweetness filled the kitchen. She loved him. Nothing else mattered—not fancy parties, not dances or beautiful dresses, not even having an elegant home.

She had felt more alive over the last couple months being with Levi than she had since she was a young girl. Peace had found her once again, and it was from being around him, which let her be her true self.

So it was decided.

After reaching for a kitchen rag, she pulled the cherry pie out of the oven. The top glistened with sugar crystals, and the leaves she'd cut out were perfectly golden brown.

With the pie in her hands, she walked into the living room. Levi's eyes lit up with hope when his gaze met hers.

"What's this?" he asked, sitting up straight.

"Do you remember that day in the cherry tree?" she asked.

A grin began to cover his face. "When I tried to kiss you?"

"Yes." She laughed and sat down next to him, setting the rag on the table, then putting the pie on top. "And I was a silly child with big dreams. I didn't know what to make of you back then."

"You were young," he said, a far-off smile on his face. He

reached for her hand. "I made my move too early, I think. You weren't ready to think of me that way."

"But I was already in love with you then," she said, shaking her head. "I didn't know what to do about it, or why you still felt like my best friend. And I made a childish choice after that to walk away from it to find something I thought was better."

Levi exhaled heavily.

"But now, here we are. I love you so much that I don't even care if you're penniless, or even if my father comes here himself to take you off to jail."

Levi shuddered. "Hopefully not."

"What I'm saying is that nothing could keep me away from you now." She stood and returned to the kitchen, bringing back two forks.

Levi took the fork she offered to him. "I'm still ashamed though. About the death."

"We'll be ashamed together. We'll wallow and eat cherry pie in the living room out of the dish."

"If I leave to go up fishing, you'll be alone. Will you be all right?" he asked, taking a bite of pie.

"I'll manage like I always have, I suppose," she replied, taking her own small bite.

The flavors were luxuriously sweet—buttery crust and warm, tart cherries.

The idea of being lonely again made her apprehensive, and the fishing boats could be dangerous. When she was younger, she'd never even imagined losing a husband in his early years, but now the possibility was real and raw. She knew how drastically things could change in a single moment, and it made her heart freeze to think of Levi surrounded by tall, angry waves off the Alaska coast.

Hopefully, it wouldn't come to that.

CHAPTER TWENTY-THREE

WATCHING THE LIGHT

ANNA

Anna woke alone in the dark tent, smelling ham and eggs cooking on the fire. From here on out, it would be mostly water, coffee, and hardtack. She had made a batch before they left—pretty much only consisting of flour, salt, and water. The other men referred to it as "sheet-iron," and she agreed. Although hers were probably better than theirs.

It wasn't something that could be eaten dry usually. It was best dipped in coffee or simply sucked on. But she had learned on the last summit that consistently eating small portions of anything, something, as she climbed made a world of difference in her energy levels.

Outside the tent, she could hear Ben and another man discussing the recently opened Seattle Public Library. Then a hearty laugh rang out and she knew it was John. She was glad Ben was already beginning to connect with the team, and she smiled as she reached for the clothes she had laid out. The pants, the white button-up shirt, and her mother's cameo brooch that had come to be one of the most special earthly possessions she owned. With great care, she fastened it at her collar, then she lifted her head high as she emerged from the tent.

"Thought you might sleep all day, princess," Lou called to her with a grin, his gray and light brown hair combed straight back.

"It's not even five in the morning, you old grump," John said, shaking his head.

She breathed a sigh of relief. "Good morning, everyone."

"We were talking about the library," John said to her. "Did you know that the owner of the newspaper I work for donated a considerable portion to the endeavor? His name's Mr. Hunt."

"And we're grateful for his contribution," she said, sitting down to join them.

Mr. Flannaghan was taking down his tent beyond the fire, and she could only assume Lou and Peter had been the ones holed up in the barn.

"We'll have a hearty breakfast, get these animals ready for the road, and then head out," he said, packing the canvas of his tent neatly and tying it with a rope.

A chickadee called from a nearby tree as Anna sat down near the fire next to Ben. The meadow grass was a golden yellow and dancing in the warm breeze. There would only be a couple more days of this warmth before they gained elevation at the base of the mountain.

Mr. Flannaghan stretched toward the sky, then put his hands on his lower back. "This may be my last trip up Rainier. I'm getting old."

"You don't look all that old," she said, giving him a warm smile.

"Well, thank you, dear," he said, then turned to the group who had all gathered around the fire. "I'll go to the animals now, and you all can eat and finish packing up."

John turned to Ben, his reddish hair catching in the sunlight. "Two or three days walking through meadows and lowlands, then we'll be at the foot of the mountain."

Ben grinned, and they all dug into the grits with crab apple jelly that had been prepared. "And how many miles will we cover in that time?"

John pushed his black-rimmed glasses up his nose without looking up from his notebook. He flipped back a few pages, then answered, "As the crow flies, it's about fifty miles, but I think we nearly double that winding through the prairies and farms. But the pack mules carry our things and it's easy walking, so the time goes quickly. Doesn't it, Anna?"

She smiled and stood, having finished her breakfast. She buckled the straps on her pack as Ben finished wrapping the canvas of their tent with rope. "Shall we, gentlemen?"

Peter huffed and took off toward the field where Mr. Flannaghan was feeding the animals.

When they were loaded up and ready to go, it wasn't even six in the morning. The sun was already warming her hair despite the refreshing coolness of the morning.

Peter and Lou took the lead with the first pony, followed by Anna, Ben, and John. Mr. Flannaghan took up the rear with the final mule.

They stopped briefly for lunch, and later that day they set up camp in an open prairie, starting a fire to prepare their dinner. One lone tree stood in the middle of the field. It was the most beautiful and lonely tree she had ever seen.

That night in their tent, she was exhausted from the day of walking. Barely able to keep her eyes open, she reached for Ben's hand. He'd been softly snoring almost from the moment he'd put his head down. As she drifted off into a deep sleep, she thought of Isabella Bird and her fiery romance with one-eyed Rocky Mountain Jim. She'd read about it in *A Lady's Life in the Rocky Mountains*. But this was even better.

The next morning, she woke before Ben, thankfully, and crept outside to begin breakfast. At least no one would be able to make fun of her for sleeping in again. Her beloved mountain loomed closer than ever, dark blue behind it and wispy white clouds around the peak, as if it were starting to steam.

She got the grits and coffee going, then Peter joined her by the fire.

"You going to get injured again?" he asked roughly.

She turned to him with a frown. "I'm sorry about what happened last time, but I'm much better prepared currently."

"You really shouldn't have come back," he whispered, glaring off toward the mountain.

Her legs tingled from the blow of his words. How dare he? She was every bit as ready for this as anyone else on the team. But before she could defend herself further, the sound of a canvas tent rustling made them both look over.

Mr. Flannaghan stepped out of his tent before she could respond. "Good morning. Ahh, thanks for starting breakfast, Anna."

Peter reached for a stake holding his tent down, pulling it up before she could say any more.

"Good morning," she said to Mr. Flannaghan.

Should she tell Ben what he'd said? She loved how well he got along with John and Mr. Flannaghan, and she wasn't sure if it was worth the bother to tell him about Peter's ugliness. After all, he wouldn't be able to come into her tent with Ben in there. And it would only make her husband angry to hear about how awful Peter was.

No, the best course of action would be to ignore Peter as she did with most of the opinions others had of her. He didn't need to like her.

They travelled even farther that day around winding creeks. A few times, she reached her hands into the ice-cold water and splashed it onto her face to cool her. It was refreshing with the summer sun beating down on them.

That day, Anna spent most of her time daydreaming about the summit while soaking up the wildlife and greenery around her. Ben and John did a lot of chatting and she joined in occasionally, but the rest of the team was somewhat spread out and less interested in conversation. After a lovely valley with white flowers, they reached Forked Creek where they would camp for the evening.

By lunchtime the next day, they reached the Succotash Valley and it was filled with wild raspberries. After they'd had their fill, they passed scattered farms. Occasionally they'd say hello to the children who would come running up to them, or wave at the parents on their porches or in the fields.

On the morning of the third day, they passed Longmire Springs, and she immediately recognized the pungent smell of sulfur.

"Well, this smell means we've come the fifty miles I was telling you about, Ben," John said, scribbling in his notebook.

"And have we gained any elevation? It's starting to feel a bit cooler." Ben lifted his face to the breeze, clearly in his element.

Mr. Flannaghan nodded importantly. "We're at two

thousand seven hundred feet now. After we pass through the Nisqually River, we'll only have ten miles to go before we reach base camp."

"I'm guessing that awful roaring sound is the Nisqually?" Ben asked.

"That it is," Lou said, tightening his belt. "Let's get everything squared away and tied down before crossing."

Anna secured her items on the mule she was walking next to, giving the grayish brown rump a pat. "Don't worry, little fella. We'll get you across safe and sound."

"There's a glacier about a mile up which is where this water's comin' from," John said, pointing up to a tall canyon.

Ben reached for her hand and squeezed it. He had not given her too many displays of affection so far as they'd decided not to make a thing of it around the team. They were able to touch each other all they wanted in their tent at night, so it was only a small sacrifice to maintain a little bodily distance during the day.

Her hand in his felt secure, and she looked toward the river with a little less anxiety. After all, she'd crossed it twice already, once on her way out and then again on their return trip. Her pants would dry soon enough after they got to the other side.

A full-size tree came tumbling down the middle of the roaring river as they reached it, and her stomach fell. The ball of roots extended into the sky on one end, the crumbling branches on the other, as it sailed by them at an incredible speed.

Lou tied a rope to a tree, then waded across the rushing river while the team watched. Once he was safely to the other side, he tied the rope to another tree.

Mr. Flannaghan had to raise his voice over the roar. "Hold on carefully to the rope and walk beside your animal. Water shouldn't reach over your waist, but the animals might try and swim. Make sure they are downriver from you in case they get pulled into a current."

Everyone obeyed, lining up and following him in.

The icy water was a shock to Anna's skin even though she'd been fully expecting it. She had to dodge a small boulder that came toward her, but it ended up hitting the rear of her mule, and the animal squealed.

"Sorry about that," she whispered.

The water did reach her waist, which chilled her all the more, but soon they were all safely on the far bank. They all sat down in the grass to pour water out of their boots.

Anna smiled, knowing her damp socks wouldn't cause nearly as much trouble as they had on her previous trip.

She gladly left the roar of the Nisqually River behind to begin their zigzag ascent up the canyon. Even with the wind being cooler than in the earlier valleys, the sun beamed down on her neck, warming her clothes and drying them in good time. She was still grateful to be in pants and not sloshing around in soaked skirts.

Soon they reached a forest of fir, spruce, and pine trees all mixed together. It was a glorious sight, the earthy smell divine. She breathed the scent in deeply, feeling at peace, knowing they had reached her mountain.

As they continued to ascend toward the Camp of the Clouds, the trees thinned, making way for sweeping swaths of wild mountain flowers. The sweet floral smells here were even more delightful, and she resisted the urge to pick a large bouquet like a child might. Maybe she would on the way down when she had nothing left to prove to the gentlemen in the group.

A large bumblebee lazily shifted from one large blue bloom

to a smaller white one. Purple lupines lined an entire hill and as the sun began to sink lower into the sky, purple hues filled the sky as well. The sun shone through wiry fir trees to the west, throwing sunbeams sparkling into the flowers.

Anna caught her breath at the beauty. Even as the group turned at the edge of the hill to make the short hike up to the base camp that was now in sight, she stood alone watching the light dance among the mountain flowers.

CHAPTER TWENTY-FOUR
ALL THAT LIES BELOW

ANNA

As she arrived at basecamp, the mountain stood closer than ever—crisp white edges against the bright blue sky. The air itself seemed thinner as the wind rustled the daisies around her feet.

She recalled John Muir's words as he'd reached the Camp of the Clouds:

> *Out of the forest at last, there stood the mountain, wholly unveiled, awful in bulk and majesty, filling all the view like a separate newborn world.*

Last year, the mountain had quickly been veiled in clouds and a light drizzle after she'd arrived, but this awe-inspiring sight was a good sign.

"This is where we leave the animals," Mr. Flannaghan

said, mostly to Ben. "There won't be any more trees for chopping down either. It's mostly ice above base camp."

Ben nodded, untying his pack atop his mule. "What will our water source be from here on up?"

"We'll fill all our water skins tonight by melting snow over the fire," Lou replied. "Then tomorrow once we make camp halfway up, we'll add snow in and leave it in the evening sun to melt a bit. Might get lucky and find running water on a glacier, but never can tell."

Ben smiled. "I'm glad you all have so much knowledge and experience."

Anna looked behind her to admire the wildflowers painted onto the side of the mountain, then turned toward the heights where great glaciers and ridges lay.

"If we leave early enough in the morning and the weather holds, we can make it halfway and make camp in time for a good night's rest," Lou said.

"I think that's a good idea," Mr. Flannaghan said. "We can spend another evening resting before the ascent."

"We'll rest this afternoon too, get to sleep early, and then leave well before morning light," Lou said, then spat by his feet and turned away.

"Well then," Mr. Flannaghan said with a shrug. "Now we make preparations and rest easy."

Anna looked to Ben. "It's not possible to get much sleep while lying on freezing ice anyway. The howling of the wind alone is nearly deafening."

Ben put his arm around her. "I'm sure it will be good to break up the ascent into two days. And today I will rest with my love and enjoy this unbelievable view."

They set up their tent near the others. There were quite a few circles of tents at the camp, and she enjoyed searching the sea of faces for anyone she might recognize from the previous year. The corrals for the mules and ponies stood at the far end, and the animals seemed to enjoy the luscious fields.

Inside their tent, she laid down next to Ben and stretched her legs out. They were certainly sore, but it was bearable, especially with minimal blisters on her feet.

He put his arm out and she laid her head on his chest, listening to the sound of his heartbeat. Even though she was purely exhausted, she knew better than to fall asleep and risk not getting proper rest that evening. She'd have a hard enough time falling asleep that night, knowing the next day would bring her to the summit.

"How are you doing?" he asked, rubbing her arm gently.

"Excited for tomorrow, but just as nervous," she replied.

"Me too." He kissed the top of her head, and then they both fell silent.

But even as she tried to rest, the pace of her heart sped up as she imagined what the summit would be like. What dangers lay between base camp and the summit? Try as they might, death could reach them at any point. Was this climb worth risking her life?

She looked over at Ben, and he leaned toward her and kissed her lips softly. As he pulled away, he smiled widely at her.

"It's going to go great. Stop worrying."

She laughed and sat up. "I'm going to take a walk around camp. Enjoy the view and the wildflowers."

"Mind if I stay here and rest?" he asked.

"As long as you promise not to sleep," she replied.

"I'll do my very best." He winked and then stretched both hands out behind his head, closing his eyes.

Outside the tent, the air was cool and sweet. She strode

toward the outskirts of the camp, admiring the flowers that were much thinner at this altitude.

A campfire to her right caught her attention, and she noticed John and Peter had joined another group, so she wandered over to say hello.

John perked up at her arrival. "And this here is Mrs. Chambers. She was in our group last year, but this will be her first summit."

Peter scoffed and spat near his feet.

Anna glared at Peter but smiled warmly at John, then she nodded a greeting at the other men around the fire.

She sat next to John and leaned in. "And I suppose I can't talk you out of writing about this attempt, can I?"

She had meant to say hello, but those words had unintentionally slipped out instead.

He seemed hurt. "I could leave you out of the story if you wish—"

"No, I'm sorry. I love that you wrote about it last year. I'm proud of what I've accomplished already. It's just that it's caused some trouble at my family's bookstore."

"Really? What kind of trouble?" He pushed his orange-red hair off his forehead with a thick hand.

"Well, there were a few times people refused to shop there," she said. "Actually, it was burned by arson a few days before we left on this trip, but I'm afraid that was. . .someone from out of town who didn't even see the article."

"I'm quite sorry to hear about that," he said. "I'd be happy to leave your name off my upcoming article if that's what you'd like. Should I leave out your husband's name as well?"

"No, neither of those things will be necessary." She sighed and looked up at the mountain, emboldened by the sheer nearness of it. "People will have to get used to it eventually. I hope to somehow start a women's mountaineering group soon, so that will make things even more official. No sense hiding out, right?"

"Well, it's entirely up to you." He stood, gathering his notebook and pen from the grass he'd been sitting in. "Maybe talk it over with Ben and see what he thinks."

She nodded but didn't mention the fact that she didn't need his permission. Or maybe John was simply suggesting she think it over and let Ben help her decide. It was hard to know if she was being overly sensitive about things, but typically people did not mean well when they said things of that nature.

After John had left the fire, she looked over at Peter, who was still staring at her with a steely gaze. It put a shot of ice through her. She could detect clear hate in his eyes.

She shuddered and looked away, leaving the group and heading back to her tent.

A light snore came from inside the tent when she arrived, and she shook her head good-naturedly. Ben never had any trouble sleeping, and he wouldn't that evening either. It wouldn't hurt to let him sleep a few more minutes before waking him.

She pulled out her compass, admiring the beautiful thing, and then she lay down next to him. They had nine thousand feet of elevation to go before reaching the steamy crater at the summit of the mountain. Lou believed they could cover that, ice and all, in two days if they left early enough. It gave her goose bumps thinking of the icy cliff faces she would encounter the next day.

Anna returned to their camp and pulled out her journal. Despite the crisp landscape and particularly lovely skies, she felt little motivation to write. She flipped back a few pages until she found a passage she had copied down from *Anna Karenina*.

He soon felt that the fulfillment of his desires gave him only one grain of the mountain of happiness he had expected. This fulfillment showed him the eternal error men make in imagining that their happiness depends on the realization of their desires.

She sighed. Summiting would certainly make her happy, but she knew there was a nugget of truth in those words, and it tugged at her.

After a time of resting, she woke Ben for dinner. Afterwards, they snuggled together to sleep, far before the sun went down.

It seemed like she'd been asleep for merely moments when Lou's gruff voice broke the silence in the darkness outside their tent.

"It's half past two. Better get movin'."

Ben rubbed his eyes and kissed her cheek before reaching for his boots.

By the light of a half-moon and countless stars, Anna helped Ben pack their things and strap the essentials onto each other's backs. It was far colder than it had been in the light of day, and she knew the sun wouldn't rise for at least another two hours. She wore the fox fur vest Heather had made for her underneath her wool coat, but she needed to get moving before she'd gain any internal heat.

She smeared coal around her cheeks and forehead as Fay had suggested the previous summer. Now that they were going to gain elevation quickly, a simple wide-brimmed hat was not going to suffice. Ben and John put some on their face as well, but the rest of the team seemed content with the protection of their hats and handkerchiefs.

There were still a handful of fires around the camp with a few men surrounding them. Likely, they had already summited or attempted it. Otherwise they'd be more concerned about their rest. One group sang a quiet song while a harmonica led the way.

Silently, the group marched forward out of the camp and toward the summit. They were immediately greeted with icy ground, the grass and daisies all but vanished. Lou led the way with Peter trailing behind to take up the rear of the group.

As she looked up at the stars, she realized the clear night sky meant they had no cloud coverage, which would prove to be quite useful. That meant no snow or even clouds to block their view as they made their ascent. They'd be able to see a storm coming if it did, and when they reached summit, the view would be indescribable.

They moved up and down over snowy hills, careful not to step into any of the chutes they'd slide down on their descent.

As dark blue seeped into the black night sky like watercolor, the majestic view came into focus. It was a truly wondrous sight, but the most awe-inspiring part was looking up at the icy slopes and peaks they had yet to climb.

She donned her darkened goggles as soon as the sun crested the mountain, shining brightly before them and bouncing rays off the ice from every direction.

A few breathtaking but tiring hours later, they reached a safe place to break for lunch.

As they ate, another group joined them—five men, all quite tall. They were on their descent.

"How's it look up there, Jim?" Lou stood and looped his thumbs through his belt loops.

"It's nice and clear at the summit, old man," said the man in the lead.

The men spent a few minutes chatting with their team and then moved on with their descent.

They didn't climb much farther that day as Lou wanted them to rest up from the steep day of climbing and replenish their water supply.

When they reached the ridge where they had camped for an evening the year before, they made camp with the minimal supplies they had been willing to carry. They pulled out hardtack to munch on, admiring the view. One mountain peak was visible to the south and another directly to the north.

Nearly in a daze from exhaustion, Anna fell into a listless sleep next to Ben, the wind howling around them.

Just before sunrise the next day, they gathered their things, along with their water skins now full again with melted snow and water.

There was a mesmerizing glow on the side of the mountain in the light of the moon. The bright stars twinkled their radiance, bringing an ethereal presence. The glaciers reflected beams of moonlight all around, and as the team set out again on their path upward, the edges of the sky turned purple.

The promise of another clear day and a reachable summit made Anna's heart soar. She knew they'd need their crampons for the next bit as it was slippery with pure ice on the peak of the Cowlitz Glacier.

As they reached the path and everyone sat down to fasten their crampons, she leaned toward Ben. "This is ten thousand feet elevation. Are you nauseated at all? I am."

"Yes, a little, but I think it might be the sight of that dark blue crevasse hundreds of feet down there."

He did look a little white in the face, but his cheeks were already pink from the sun.

An hour later, they reached Cathedral Gap, where they removed their crampons and crunched through loose rocks and pebbles. Anna was careful to hold tightly to her alpenstock through her gloved fingers to secure her footing. The new gloves she and Ben had purchased had holes for their fingers and thumbs for exactly this purpose.

And as soon as they had appeared, the rocks disappeared in favor of more ice. With crampons back on their feet, Lou roped them all together.

"I'm sick of being the caboose on this train," Peter whined.

"I don't mind taking up the rear," Ben said.

Lou shrugged and put Anna in front of him and then Peter. She was grateful for the order, which meant she could turn and smile at Ben as often as she wanted to without seeing Peter glare at her.

As the group began to move, she turned back to Ben, who was about ten feet behind her, and lowered her voice. "The Ingraham Glacier is next. This is the spot where I twisted my ankle."

He nodded knowingly.

The weather remained fine and no avalanches presented themselves, so they kept a steady pace, but it was none too quick. She couldn't figure for certain exactly where she'd stepped on the hidden boulder the year before, but when she had reached new ground, she knew it was behind her.

Lou turned from his place in the front and shouted something to the group. With the wind howling, she couldn't be certain what he'd said.

"Peter, what did he say?" Anna asked.

"On your hands and knees now," Peter replied.

"Excuse me?"

"Oh don't flatter yourself," he said with disgust. "We have to crawl along this part. You wouldn't know because you didn't make it this far last time."

Her face burned with anger and embarrassment. Ben shook his head at her as if to say to ignore him. They both assumed a crawling position, made even more awkward as they were roped together and still wearing their crampons.

The slope was steep, but there were mounds and miniature peaks in the landscape on which to gain footholds.

In front of her, Peter took a seat and pulled out his canteen. None of the others had paused, so she kept moving toward him, expecting him to start again before she got to him.

But when she reached his position, he turned around and put a knife to her stomach.

Anna gasped, but Peter slapped a hand over her mouth. Ben was still ten feet below with a boulder in between that blocked his view of what was happening.

"Burning down your bookstore wasn't enough of a hint, eh?" He was inches away from her face, where his gloved hand was making it hard for her to breathe. "You got no place up here."

The jolt of realization made her even more light-headed. The pressure of his knife against her coat was sickening. Then he suddenly reached up to the rope, cut it just behind him, and shoved her as hard as he could down the mountain.

CHAPTER TWENTY-FIVE

ATTEMPTED MURDER

ANNA

The air was knocked from Anna's lungs as she hit the ice below her. As she slid down the mountain, the rope still connected to Ben tightened, pulling him down behind her.

She struggled to breathe—as if her lungs had been removed from her body. The muscles in her chest forgot how to draw a breath, and the panic of careening down the mountain was nothing compared to the desperate lack of oxygen.

What seemed like an eternity later, she took in the tumble of the world around her. She was able to draw in a first inhale and plunged her alpenstock into the ice as hard as she could.

She figured they must have slid a hundred feet or more. Ben was above her slightly on the mountain, also with his alpenstock stuck deeply in the ice. He must have been doing it before she had, slowing their descent. What would have happened if she'd lost consciousness? They might have both plunged to their deaths with her dead weight dragging them down the mountain.

That must have been exactly Peter's plan. It would have looked like an accident to the group. The rope might have been frayed or got snagged against a sharp rocky ledge, and the two people at the bottom of the train might easily fall to their deaths with no other safety net in place.

She stuck the blades of one boot and then the other against the slippery ice, gaining a foothold. Ben was already climbing down toward her.

"You all right?" he called.

She nodded, anger seeping out of her veins until she was hot all over. "It was Peter."

"Did he fall too? Should we go up and check on him?" Dark red blood trickled down the left side of his forehead.

"No. He did this on purpose. And he's the one who burned the bookstore."

Ben stared at her without understanding, his eyes dazed. He reached up to wipe the blood away from his forehead and then looked down at his hand with curiosity.

"Are *you* all right?" She reached up to brush his hair away from the blood.

"How can you be sure?" he asked softly.

His eyes were darting from one place on the horizon to the other. He must have been thinking through the turn of events. Yelling at his father, then storming away. They had both come to the same conclusion on their own—it had seemed the most likely.

"He said so," she replied, tears brimming in the corners of her eyes. "He said I don't belong up here and that burning down the store must not have been enough."

Ben reached for her and took her in his arms, then looked

above them for Peter. He scooted them both under an icy ledge and out of sight from above. "As long as you're safe, everything is fine."

"But what about you?" She pulled away to examine his head. "Did you hit your head on a rock?"

"It seems that way," he said, wiping at his forehead again. "It doesn't hurt though, and I feel fine. Just a little disoriented from the fall. And we'll probably both be sore tomorrow."

He looked up toward the summit again. "Do you suppose they're going to come back down for us?"

She shook her head. "I imagine Peter told them we plummeted to our deaths and our bodies couldn't be recovered. If he can see us now, he'll probably try to unsettle a chunk of ice above us to come crashing down to finish the job."

Anger flashed white-hot in her mind, and she could feel an ache in her jaw as her teeth began to grind together.

"Well, let's wait a bit until they're far enough ahead and then meet them at the summit," he replied, a twinkle in his eye.

A fierce determination filled her as she pulled away from him and turned toward the summit. What a confrontation was in store for that horrid man.

The rope that still held them together was secure, and they both still had their alpenstocks and an ice ax each. Slowly and carefully, they began the climb once again through snowless ice.

It seemed as if the mountain itself had set traps for ambitious climbers in the form of yawning canyons of ice— scars on the face of the slopes—as if tears of fire had dripped down her summit.

Anna stopped in front of what looked like a frozen log over a canyon. "A snow bridge. That's what Muir called it."

"That looks. . .dangerous." Ben stepped up behind her, the rope lagging between them.

"We need to test it first." She looked around for anything heavy—a small boulder maybe.

But Ben got onto all fours and crawled toward the bridge of ice covered in snow. His nearness to the edge made Anna's stomach drop. She anchored herself as best she could with her alpenstock.

Once he got to the bridge, he lowered himself onto his stomach and moved forward inch by inch, testing the depth of the snow covering the ice with his ice ax.

Slowly, he shuffled across while she stayed anchored with her alpenstock. When he got to the other side, he anchored himself while she crawled over.

Once they were both safely on the other side, Anna blew out a relieved breath.

"I wonder if we've gotten off the path the others were on," she said, holding her hand to shade her eyes. Even the dark goggles couldn't soften the glare the sun made of the brilliant white all around them.

He pointed at the ice where crampon tracks marked the way. "That's either their tracks or the other team's. Either way, we're nearly there. I reckon we keep heading upward." The bleeding near his eyebrow had mostly stopped. "You don't mind if I kill Peter when we reach the top, right?"

She laughed nervously. "I think that's my job."

She bit her lip. Surely, he'd lied to the rest of the group and would continue to do so. It would be their word against his. They certainly couldn't just attack him on sight.

"I'm going to kill him," Ben said without a hint of amusement.

"Mr. Flannaghan will believe us. And John."

Ben shook his head and started moving toward the final ridge. "I'll climb up a bit and then secure my ax. You come after. Make sure to place your spikes directly down into the ice as you go."

"You mean I shouldn't step on any boulders?" she asked coolly.

"That's not what I meant. Just easy does it, all right?"

She had never seen his face so consumed with nervous energy, not even when he'd asked her to marry him. Although he probably knew that was a sure thing. Everything they'd been training for was down to these last twenty minutes or so, and then what? A confrontation on the summit? Who knew if their group would even still be there. She'd heard of groups staying in the crater for less than two hours before returning to base camp. Seemed like a waste when they could spend the day there. But now she wasn't so sure about the kind of company they might have.

"I'm sorry," he said with a strong exhale. His breath seemed labored and Anna noticed her own shortness of breath in the thin air, despite all their physical training.

He pulled her into an embrace, then he lifted her chin and kissed her. It was a soft, reassuring kiss, and it was exactly what she needed—a feeling of belonging and empowerment.

"I'm angry and I'm apprehensive about this last part. But you and me—we can do this."

"Absolutely. We'll do it together." She smiled up at him.

After that, her spirit was buoyed with joy and a peace she hadn't experienced since the last time she'd been on the mountain—*their* mountain.

She cautiously put one bladed foot in front of the other. Nausea had been creeping in on her along with a pounding in her head. Being this high in the sky didn't come without effects on the body.

"Do you feel ill at all?" she asked Ben.

"Well, I didn't want to complain, but I feel my breath is shallower since we left base camp. And the idea of eating anything sounds downright awful. Must be the altitude, eh?"

She nodded, thinking the same way about food. Which reminded her that they should drink water. After taking in as much as she could, she passed the water skin to Ben.

As they kept moving forward higher and higher, she finally saw rocks above her, a stark contrast from the blinding snow and ice. They hurried to reach them.

And then finally she took the last step that brought her to the moment she'd been waiting for since she was a little girl.

Two craters lay at the top of the mountain, but she was more interested in the view beyond them. Through the crystal-clear sky, she could see Mount St. Helen's and Mount Adams to the south. A little farther in the distance, she thought she could even see Mount Hood.

She smiled up at Ben and put her arm around his waist. What pure joy it was to have accomplished her goal. But then she realized they hadn't actually reached the highest point of the mountain.

"To summit, I believe we need to walk across the crater and climb to that crest. It's probably where the rest of the team is."

Hand in gloved hand, they walked through the expanse of what was clearly a volcanic crater. It was less windy inside the safety of the bowl. There were pockets of warm air blowing out of steam vents.

"We could melt some snow with this warm air, and then warm our hands," Ben suggested.

Both of those ideas sounded wonderful to Anna, and she felt no rush to meet up with their team.

He scooped snow into their water skins that still contained some water, and they swirled them over the warm steam until only water remained.

After taking long drinks, they took off their gloves and warmed their hands. It brought feeling back all the way to her toes as if she were in front of a fire.

Just then, a shout sounded in the distance.

"Ben! Anna!" It was John's voice.

She whirled around at once to see him waving his arms like a madman with a goofy grin on his face.

"You're all right! I can't believe it," he said as he reached them.

"Where is everyone?" she asked, putting her gloves back on.

"They're just at the bottom of the crest. Made camp for the night and enjoyin' the view." He lowered his eyes with a hint of guilt. "Mr. Flannaghan and I wanted to head back for you both, but Peter was certain he saw you both fall into a crevasse too far down the mountain. I'm awfully sorry——"

"He lied," Ben said, folding his arms. "He put a knife to Anna, cut our rope loose, then shoved her down the mountain. He tried to kill us both."

John gasped, putting a hand to his mouth. "Well, that's. . . That's. . .attempted murder!"

CHAPTER TWENTY-SIX

SAY YES

EMILY

After the afternoon eating cherry pie with Levi, Emily had been resolute in her decision to love him unconditionally for the rest of her life. He hadn't even asked for her hand in marriage yet, but her heart was already forever his.

Her debt would be paid in full in a few months, and she already felt like a new woman. Now, all she could think about was a new life with Levi, whether she had to keep working at the grocer or not, whether they would struggle to make ends meet their whole lives or not. He was home to her.

The only truly disappointing part would be that he was leaving to go fishing and she'd be alone for a few months. And that would likely be the case every spring. But having him with her the rest of the time would make the sacrifice worth it.

She sighed and shut the door behind her as she got ready to walk to the Gallagher house for dinner. Long summer walks had become more enjoyable over the last couple of months, especially when Levi walked her home in the warm evenings.

When she arrived, he greeted her with a kiss on her cheek and ushered her inside to sit beside him at the fireplace. All the windows in the house were open, and a delightful cross breeze blew around, mixing with the warmth of the small fire in the living room.

"Good afternoon, Emily," Greta chimed from the kitchen. "Oscar and I are going to take a stroll into town for sugar for the ice cream I'm going to make. Would you two like to join us?"

"She just walked all the way here," Levi said. "You both go ahead, and we'll keep an eye on the roast."

Greta put her hands on her hips. "You behave yourself, Levi."

He laughed, but then his face assumed a grave yet ironically serious expression. "Yes, ma'am."

Emily felt a warm blush cover her cheeks, and she shook her head at Greta.

After they had left, he pulled his chair closer to her. "What sort of trouble should we get into?"

She laughed and stood to walk toward the kitchen. "I think we have the very important task of watching a chicken roast slowly in the cookstove."

The way he watched her move sent shivers down her spine. He stood slowly, eyes not leaving hers. When he took her hand, the warmth of the touch made her relax, and she let him pull her close.

He pushed her gently against the wall, releasing her hand to put both of his palms on her cheeks. His gaze shifted from her eyes and down toward her mouth, and then the force of years of attraction brought them together.

The kiss was sweet at first, but then she could feel heat building in her chest. He pulled away suddenly, out of breath and looking at her in awe.

"Something tells me that if I'd kissed you in the cherry tree that day, it wouldn't have been that amazing."

The sound of horses galloping up the dirt drive made them both look toward the door. Outside, a fine coach was nearing the Gallagher house, two white horses carrying it.

By the time it arrived at the front, Emily and Levi had already moved to the porch where the sun shone down around them. She was thankful for the distraction from the empty house and the powerful kiss. Although she was already looking forward to the next private kiss.

The door of the coach opened before the horses stopped, and Mr. Yesler himself jumped to the ground with a thud, much to the driver's clear dismay.

"Mr. Gallagher," Yesler said, his voice loud and sure of himself. "What's this I hear of you quitting?"

"I stepped down, sir," Levi replied, taking his hands out of his pockets as if needing to defend himself.

"On account of the accident?" Yesler asked, cocking his head to the side.

"Uh, yes, sir." Levi crossed his arms over his chest resolutely, but Emily could see the guilt creeping into his expression.

"Well, every man who was present says it was a true and honest accident the fellow made. Wasn't your fault, son."

Levi was silent for a beat and then shook his head. "But I was in charge, and I feel responsible."

Yesler took off his hat and looked up at the sky, wiping a layer of sweat from his forehead. "The mill can be a dangerous place to work. And being in charge of other men there can be a great responsibility. But some men have to do it, and I like you, son."

Levi blinked, his Adam's apple moving as if he'd swallowed back his surprise.

"And your team misses you something fierce. They don't want a new manager. They want you to come back. We all do. What do ya say?"

Levi fought a grin and Emily took his hand, looking up at him questioningly.

"Before I agree, may I have a moment to speak with my girl?" Levi asked, winking down at her.

"Right, right." Yesler pulled out a cigar and lit it, leaning his back against the coach.

Once inside the house, a grin spread over Levi's face like the sun rising. "What do you think, Em?"

"If that's what you want, you should say yes," she said. "But I don't want you to do it for me, all right? I want you to choose what will make you happy."

"You mean besides having you to come home to every day?" He grinned. "What if we— I mean, it'd be nice to take some time off at some point. If we. . ."

He cleared his throat and then grabbed her hand. They walked as one back to where the older man stood.

Levi leaned down and whispered, "Don't let this scare you, but I'm going to ask about time off for a honeymoon."

She caught her breath, but he kept his eyes coolly on Yesler. She squeezed his hand.

"About how much time might I be able to take off for a honeymoon? I mean, whenever the time is right."

Yesler howled with laughter. "As much as you need, son. So long as you come straight back to the mill first thing on the morrow."

The grin on Levi's face made her heart soar. As he nodded and waved good-bye to Yesler, he looked like a boy, proud to start work again and spend time with a man he respected. He'd be honored to have his position back in order to provide for the family they would have one day.

As they stood hand in hand watching the fancy coach and white horses ride away in the summer heat, Emily's heart was full—full of peace, happiness, and hope for the future.

CHAPTER TWENTY-SEVEN
A BEAUTIFUL CONSEQUENCE

ANNA

Anna watched John and Ben exchange a knowing glance. "I'm definitely on your side, Ben," John said. "And we'll get him to the jailhouse as soon as we reach Yelm. But I wouldn't recommend doing anything rash."

Ben scoffed and pushed past both of them, walking toward the crest of the mountain.

The other men must have heard the shouting, because Mr. Flannaghan and Lou appeared a moment later with relief written on their faces.

When Mr. Flannaghan reached Anna, he embraced her with tears in his eyes. "My dear, you're all right. I've been a ball of nerves since you slipped away from us."

After explaining the truth to him and Lou, she watched their faces turn to disgust.

"D'ya swear, Anna?" Lou asked. "Promise me that's how it happened, and I'll throw Peter off this mountain right now."

There was still a raging torrent of anger in her chest, but she didn't want anyone to die that day. "It's the truth, Lou. Let me speak with him, please."

"I'll tie him up first," Lou said, spitting near his feet.

When they reached the makeshift summit camp, they found it deserted.

"He's hiding," John said apprehensively, pushing his glasses up his nose while looking around the craters.

"He's a yella belly, and he already started his descent," Lou said. "His gear's gone."

Ben's tense posture loosened. After a moment's pause, he said, "Good riddance to him. Let's enjoy this glorious summit."

"Don't worry, Anna," John said. "We'll all testify for ya. And I'll write it exactly as it happened. What a story!"

"I'm bettin' he's headed for Oregon, maybe even California," Lou said, shaking his head. "Shameful creature. I thought I knew him better than that."

"Quite right," Mr. Flannaghan said. "Let's do enjoy this exquisite view. Last year, there was such expansive cloud coverage. We could barely see Seattle, let alone the Cascades. Are you ready to reach the summit, Anna?"

With swelling pride, Anna grinned and they all climbed up the rocky scramble to reach the very highest point on the mountain.

The craters steamed below them, and the sharp smell of boiled eggs hung in the air, just as it had near the soda springs at the foot of the mountain.

All the fear and doubt had been worth it. Nothing in her life up to that point had been better than the exhilaration she felt in that moment. The weather, the circumstances, the mountain itself had seemed to give approval that she should reach the top. In light of the summit, she couldn't imagine anything ever feeling so beautiful.

Ben put an arm around her. "I'm not so sure about putting our feet in those springs in the crater."

Anna laughed. "I don't think I'd like to drink that water either."

"I can draw you a bath at home any time you like."

"Not with these views," she said, looking up at a few clouds that had come rolling in.

"We can see hundreds of miles," Ben said with awe. "I think I can see our house."

She laughed. "Of course you can't see our house!"

"Okay, not really," he said with a grin. "But I can see the Sound and ships moored at the dock. That's our city, Anna."

They all spent the evening telling stories about the various training they each had completed and what adventures they hoped to take in the future.

By the time night had fallen, Anna's muscles ached with fatigue. They'd been up for nearly twenty hours and had scaled a mountain to boot.

With her feet out of the water, the icy winds blew strong and she curled up next to Ben for the night.

As soon as the sun rose the next day, they began their descent. By the time they reached base camp, there was no sign of Peter, and no one had seen him either. There was a missing mule though, and John scribbled this fact down in his notebook with perhaps too much enthusiasm.

A tall man with a black hat approached Anna. "Ma'am, are you Anna Gallagher?"

"Yes," she replied. "Well, it's Anna Chambers now."

He nodded. "Ms. Fuller left this letter for you. She was up here two weeks ago and was hoping you would be too. She said she didn't know how else to reach you, but it was important."

She thanked him, and then the man tipped his hat and strode away. With trembling hands, she tore open the white envelope.

Dear Miss Gallagher,

There are so few of us mountaineering women that I thought it would be good for us to get together and make plans for the future. I'm sure there must be more women who would like to climb mountains. I think it's up to us to find them and encourage the adventure inside them. I hope this letter finds you back on the mountain, and if it does, I'll know that you are the determined spirit that I believe you are. Please write me back to my home in Yelm as soon as you are able, and let me know your thoughts.

Yours on the mountain,
Fay Fuller

Anna smiled widely and handed the letter to Ben, although he'd been reading it over her shoulder.

"I should write her back as soon as we can find paper and a pencil," she said with satisfaction.

A women's mountaineering group—how delightful that she and Fay had both been pondering the same endeavor. Surely, it was meant to be—and surely, it would ruffle some feathers. It made it easier to be less afraid of people like Peter when there was a whole group of strong women fighting for each other and their right to belong on the mountain.

In the shelter of their own tent, Ben finally put his head in his hands and groaned.

"My father," he said softly.

She kneeled down next to him and put an arm around his shoulders. "I know. I keep thinking about that as well. We'll write to him immediately."

He stayed silent, but when he finally lifted his eyes to hers, tears glistened in them. "No. I need to go to him. He may have bad opinions about what women are capable of, but I've accused him of something terrible, and that can't be undone with a letter."

"Then I'll go with you," she said. "I mean, if you'd like."

"I would love that," he replied. "And you can visit June while we're there."

"That's a beautiful consequence of this whole debacle." She grinned and then kissed his cheek.

"We should go there at once, if you don't mind," he said. "We can get new clothes on the way."

She nodded with surprise, not realizing until that moment that their next adventure would be so closely following this one.

He stood, reaching down his hand to help her up. "Let's enjoy this view as long as we can. What do you say?"

She grinned and agreed, then they found a flat boulder on which to rest as they soaked in the magnificent sights below them.

CHAPTER TWENTY-EIGHT

THE SAILBOAT

EMILY

The hot August sun pressed down on Emily's back as she walked to work at Grayson's Grocer. She'd been meaning to find a new place of employment. It was quite unpleasant to work for the man whose daughter used to court the man who loved her. And it would be only a matter of time before he found out.

As she rounded the corner and entered the store, Mr. Grayson looked up with a harried expression.

"Is it true that Levi Gallagher is courting you?" he asked, putting his hands on the counter in front of him.

The blood drained from her face as she stopped abruptly.

"Yes, sir. I'm sorry. I suppose I should have said something."

He huffed. "Elizabeth'll be just fine. But it might be a good idea for you to find different employment before she returns from her aunt's."

"Of course. I understand."

She wasn't sure if she should leave at once or if he wanted her to stay for her shift. Mercifully, he had an answer for that without her having to ask.

"Your father stopped by. He said to go and meet him at the harbor."

"This morning? Is everything all right?" she asked, catching her breath.

He shrugged. "Sounded important."

She nodded and nearly tripped on her skirts as she ran out the door. Her heart pounded and her mind went from embarrassment to worry as she thought through every possible bad thing that could have happened. Why was she meeting him at the harbor? Perhaps her mother was ill and needed to be transported somewhere in a hurry.

Everyone seemed to get in her way as she hurried toward the docks. She slipped between a tram and a horse-drawn carriage to cross Front Street and ignored the driver's irritated expression.

Had there been another accident at the mill? Or had they opened an investigation after all about the accident that had taken place on Levi's team? She was nearly in tears by the time she finally reached the harbor, but it was then that she realized she had no idea where to go from there.

The docks were alive with the calls of fishermen and workers loading and unloading wagons to transport goods. Even the seagulls added to the ruckus, which made her mind spin even more.

Just as she was about to cry out in desperation, she felt a tap on her shoulder. She spun around to see her father, a serene look on his face that confused her all the more.

"There's something special planned for you, but I don't

want to ruin it by talking. May I escort you to the boat?"

"Something special? Everything is fine, then? I was troubled by Mr. Grayson's tone."

He nodded and offered his arm. "Everything's just fine. I promise."

With a deep sigh, she took his arm and wiped a tear away before it fell. She was still catching her breath and adrenaline was coursing through her, making it difficult to believe him.

"Why are we going to a boat?"

He glanced at her sidelong, trying to hide a smile. "I'm afraid it's a secret, my dear."

Now that she truly knew that nothing was wrong, her curiosity began to run wild and she immediately thought of Levi.

A moment later, they turned a corner to find a sailboat with her mother, sister, and Levi on the deck. He was wearing a fine suit and holding a bouquet of white flowers. Emily's heart leapt so hard in her chest it made her legs weak. The sight was at once stunning and hopeful, which made emotions well up inside her.

"What in the world is going on?" she asked Levi as he came forward to help her step onto the deck.

He handed off the bouquet to her mother and then took her hand.

"I know I'm going out on a limb here, but would you like to go for a sail around the harbor?"

She nodded with a smile she couldn't contain and glanced over at her mother, who was trying to hide her tears.

He led her over to her mother and sister as a few men untied the ropes and the vessel moved out into the water. Greta and Oscar were there too, which made her heart race, knowing it was indeed a special moment.

"What are you all doing here?" she asked, hugging her mother tightly.

"I think you need to check in with the man who set this all up," the older woman replied.

Levi nodded, a blush coming over his face. "Let's talk privately."

As they moved toward the back of the boat, the sails were released and the wind caught, taking them away from the city.

He leaned down to kiss her softly, and she didn't even worry that her family was nearby. The moment was so magical that nothing in all the world could ruin it.

"I know this might seem sudden, but I've loved you for as long as I can remember. And now that we're finally united, I don't ever want to let you go."

He pulled out a gold ring with a small sparkling diamond and she gasped, even though it was the thing her heart had most hoped for.

"Remember when I picked up that nugget while trying my hand at mining for gold? Even then, I hoped that you would be my wife. Even when you married Charles and I couldn't see a way for us, I still held out hope that one day you would see me the way I see you."

She wiped a tear away, her chest aching with love for the man who had just taken a knee before her.

"Emily, will you marry me?"

"Yes!" She fell to her knees along with him and they kissed again, this time longer than before.

"I actually have one more question," he said, blowing out a nervous breath. "Will you marry me today at sea?"

Now she was completely speechless.

"It's absolutely fine if the answer to that last question is no.

If you want to have a special ceremony with your friends, or if you need more time—"

"Of course I'll marry you today. I'm just stunned with all of this." Emily put her hand in his and they both stood.

Her heart fluttered, and her family came around the corner as if they'd been listening the whole time and were just waiting for this moment.

"Congratulations, darling," her mother said, tears flowing freely now. "We're delighted to be here for this."

Lauren smiled coyly at her, handing her a small suitcase. "I brought your new dress and some other things you might need to get ready. Can't have you getting married in calico."

Emily laughed for the first time all day, and the release of emotions made her light-headed. It wasn't quite her dream to be married on a boat with no preparation, but she'd already had her dream wedding with Charles. It had been over the top and exquisite, and she'd been at the height of anxiety and nerves. There had been nothing about that day which had felt peaceful.

But this day—with the deep blue ocean, the warm sea breeze, and her absolute favorite people surrounding her— may be the most perfect wedding day with Levi she could have imagined. The second chance she'd only recently dared to dream of.

With a kiss to her new fiancé, she joined her mother and sister below deck in the captain's quarters to prepare for the ceremony. Lauren had brought everything she might possibly need, including the gorgeous gown her mother had bought for her for the dance with Levi.

"How are you feeling about everything?" her sister asked her. "Is there any part of you that would rather wait, because if you'd rather—"

"This is truly perfect," she said, feeling peace like a light shawl around her shoulders. "Marrying Levi today means that I can go home with him tonight, and there's nothing I want more."

"Then let's get you ready," her mother said, reaching into the bag. "We've got new shoes for you, as well as a veil and my pearls."

In no time at all, she had transformed into what felt like a princess going to a coronation. Her mother had fashioned her hair with flowers and the lovely white veil.

When she emerged from below deck, Levi stood eagerly waiting and his jaw dropped in the most perfect way.

"You look as lovely as I've ever seen you," he said, eyes misty.

One of the sailors began to play a soft song on his guitar, and the reverend who had been invited performed a quick ceremony, uniting them as husband and wife. The wind tried its best to ruin her beautiful updo, loosing curls in its rush, but Emily didn't care. She and Levi stood at the front of the boat with a view of the entire city and the mountain beyond.

And when the ceremony was over, he kissed her softly and then scooped her into his arms, which made everyone clap and hoot.

"You know it's tradition in weddings at sea that the bride is thrown overboard after saying her vows," he said, walking toward the edge.

She scrambled to free herself, but then he winked.

"I'm just teasing."

And then he kissed her like he really meant it, and she couldn't wait to be with her best friend for the rest of their lives.

EPILOGUE
AN UNSTOPPABLE FORCE

ANNA

I n Yelm, Anna sent two telegrams. One to Greta letting her know that they would be gone another two weeks.

QUICK VISIT TO BEN'S PARENTS. TELL HEATHER. STOP.

The other, she sent to June.

UNEXPECTED VISIT. WILL ARRIVE THURSDAY AT NOON. STOP.

June and Connor now lived in San Francisco, and Ben's parents still lived in Berkeley, so they happened to be quite close.

There were precious few shops in Yelm, so after leaving their climbing gear with a friendly shop keeper, they boarded straight away after purchasing their tickets and sending the telegrams. In Astoria, they stopped to purchase a fresh change of clothes for both of them, to bathe, and to wash the clothes they'd been wearing.

When Anna stepped out of the bath with clean hair, it was a marvelous feeling indeed. She had bought a deep purple dress with white piping along the hem that made her feel sophisticated. Not only had she climbed a mountain all the way to the top, but she was also a member of the Ladies Library Association, and she'd be a founding member of the new women's mountaineering group.

She held her head high as they boarded the southbound train. There wasn't a need to be only one thing in this new day and age. She was many things: a woman, a mountaineer, a wife, a trailblazer, and, maybe one day, a mother. But even though some people believed some of those things should contradict each other, she knew that her life was exactly how it ought to be.

She just hoped that Ben's parents could not only accept her for who she was but also forgive her and Ben for jumping to conclusions.

His mother seemed to be a reasonable woman, but she was not the one Ben had accused. Dr. Chambers had made it abundantly clear that he thought very little of Anna's outdoor pursuits, but now they needed to come back to him from a position of apology. It was quite the tight rope to walk.

It would be June who would meet them at the train station. After another three days of traveling, she'd need another bath and a place to wash her new dress. It wouldn't do to speak with Ben's parents looking like road-traveled vagabonds and stinking of too many people crammed together for days.

When they settled back into the train in Astoria, she laid her head on Ben's shoulder.

"I'm relieved that it wasn't your father," she said. "I feel as if I need to get to know your parents all over again."

"Well, I'm glad I have another few days to think because, as of right now, I haven't a clue what I'm going to say. 'I'm sorry I thought you were capable of arson?'"

She looked up at him. "Yes, perhaps you should keep working on that speech."

He laughed and kissed her forehead.

Miles and miles of tall forests stretched before them with only a few cities dotting the countryside. The chugging of the steam engine was a rhythmic lull as they wound through valleys and hills.

And all the while, Ben was mostly quiet, looking out the window and pondering just how he might make amends with his parents. Sometimes, he would make a comment or ask a question and she would do her best to help, but it seemed to be something he needed to work through on his own.

When they pulled into the station in San Francisco, Anna could see June waving wildly, a chubby blond toddler on her hip.

The air was shockingly hot against her skin, which made her sweat even more. It would be good to have an afternoon and evening to freshen up and rest before surprising Ben's parents in the same way they had surprised them.

"Fancy seeing you two all the way down here," June said, shifting Joseph to her other hip. Her hair was swept up neatly in a chignon, and her yellow dress rustled softly in the hot breeze blowing in from the ocean.

Anna hugged her friend. "Thank you for meeting us. If you don't mind, I'd love to bathe and wash this dress. We plan to find Ben's parents first thing tomorrow morning. Perhaps before it gets this hot again."

June smiled at Ben, who was carrying the small bag they had brought. "How did the summit attempt go? Did you make it?"

"Oh! Yes, we did. It was incredible." Anna couldn't believe she'd forgotten to mention that first thing. She'd had a great deal on her mind since then, but it felt fantastic to share the news.

"I'll be. I'm awfully proud of you," June said. "Let's hop in one of these trams, and I'll take you to our house."

Inside the streetcar, the rushing wind gave only a slight reprieve from the unbelievable heat. It was something Anna had never experienced, and she didn't love it. Give her all the cold forests and icy mountains and she was a happy lady, but this dry, dusty heat was for the birds. June signaled to them and then hopped off on a busy street, guiding them past a horse-drawn carriage that had no intentions of slowing down.

"Connor's in his office workin' now, but he'll be home this evening." June stopped in front of a bright yellow door and then pushed it open.

Inside, the house smelled of baking bread, and it seemed even hotter than outside. June set Joseph down, and he toddled over to a wooden rocking chair just his size.

"How old is he now?" Anna asked, fanning herself with a letter that was sitting on the table.

"Just a couple months past his first birthday. He's climbing all over everything, and his energy knows no bounds."

Anna laughed and walked over to the boy. She put a hand on his soft fluffy hair, delighted that it felt nearly the same as when he was a newborn.

"I'll draw you a bath first thing. I'm guessin' you don't want it so hot, what with all this heat."

"That sounds lovely, thank you."

Ben leaned toward her and whispered, "If June had a dress you could borrow, would you mind heading over to visit my parents this evening?"

The idea of seeing them so suddenly put a knot in her stomach, but she nodded. It was clear that he wanted to get the whole business behind him as soon as possible, and she respected that. It must feel awful to have that pressure.

After Anna's bath, June helped her into a satin blue dress with white lace on the waist and collar.

"What a high collar your dress has," Anna said with a smile.

June threw her head back and laughed merrily. "I quite like not having my breasts pushed up into my neck at all times. I'm a lady now, you know."

"You've always been a lady."

"Thank you," June said, blushing slightly.

When the day had finally cooled to a reasonably warm temperature and the sun started to set behind the city buildings, they made their way toward the place Ben remembered living in long ago.

The house was elegant from the outside, with ivy crawling along the white-paneled front and reaching the second floor. Roses of pink and yellow surrounded the terrace. Their aroma was inviting.

"Ready?" Anna asked, putting her hand in his.

He nodded and reached up to knock on the door with the regal metal knocker in the shape of a lion's head.

A maid answered at once and led them into a parlor with marble floors and a large bay window that was wide open to cool the room. Wispy white curtains moved slightly in the breeze.

Anna squeezed his hand, and they both walked over to the window.

"I feel like a little boy in this house, even though I was a man when I left."

Someone cleared their throat in the entryway, and they both spun around to see his father standing in a suit with a pipe in his mouth.

"Son," he said with surprise. "I had no idea— I hardly believed the maid when she said so."

"Father, I owe you an apology." Ben let go of Anna's hand and strode toward his father. "I treated you terribly, and you didn't deserve it."

Dr. Chambers tilted his head sideways, his pipe still hanging from his mouth. "And what say you, Miss Anna?"

She swallowed hard and took a few steps toward them. "Both of us are awfully sorry for the accusation. Truly, we didn't know what to think, and after. . . Well, with your strong opinions of my expeditions. . ."

Dr. Chambers chuckled softly. "Well, now I owe you both an apology. I guess I wanted to see you squirm a little just now."

Anna frowned but felt a softening for the man. "So you forgive us?"

"Of course I do," he said, putting his arm around Ben. "My only son and his bizarre wife. I'll always love you both."

Ben breathed out a sigh of relief as a half-smile grew on his face. "You have always had the oddest sense of humor."

"We never did seem to click in that way, did we, boy?"

At that moment, Ben's mother came flying into the room with tears streaming down her face. "Oh, my son! I'm overjoyed to see you."

After she released him, she looked over to Anna. "How did it go? Did you make it to the top this time?"

Anna nodded with a grin. "Yes, ma'am, we did. We also discovered the real culprit who caused all the damage to the bookstore."

"Well, that's a relief," she said, wiping away her tears.

"If you really thought I had burned down your wife's bookstore, you ought to have punched me in the face, son."

Ben chuckled. "Is that so?"

"And anyway, if I had truly disapproved so much, I would have been more successful at stopping you both, don't you think? How would burning down the family bookstore stop you both from summiting?"

He was right, of course. It was a thought Anna had vaguely touched on, but it was Ben, after all, who had rushed to blame his father. She looked over at him expectantly, wondering what he might say.

He shrugged and lowered his head. "It's just been so long, and I guess I was afraid—unsure how much I could trust you. Unsure if you still held a grudge against me for disappearing and cutting ties."

His father grinned and gave him a rough pat on the back. "Well, it means a lot that you've both come down here now to straighten it all out. Never thought you'd end up back here, did you?"

Now it was Ben's turn to smile. "No, I did not."

His mother put an arm around Anna's waist. "How about we go out tonight and see that play we promised you?"

After the plans were made, Ben's parents hurried away to get ready, leaving the two of them in the parlor to relax for a moment. Anna plopped onto an overstuffed leather chair and sighed deeply.

"How are you feeling?" she asked.

Ben nodded slowly. "It wasn't exactly as I imagined it, but I do feel quite a relief. I think just the act of coming here as soon as we found out was something I needed to do."

"I agree. You didn't waste a moment, and I'm sure your father appreciates that." She stood to join him near the window where the twilight began to take over the sky. The dim city street lights flickered outside.

"Are you ready to see your first play, Mrs. Chambers?" He put an arm around her shoulders and drew her close.

"I'd go anywhere with you," she replied. "Even to the theater on a muggy evening with your odd father."

He laughed. "I think he likes you. You're growing on him, I can tell."

She shrugged and lifted her chin. "I know I can't please everyone, but I think I've turned out to be a woman of many talents, and I quite like going back and forth between mountain climbing and sophisticated events."

He kissed her softly and then pulled away to brush a strand of her dark hair behind her ear. "You are an unstoppable force and a beauty. I'm honored to spend my life with you."

She smiled as the evening breeze blew in, finally cooling her. She had much to put in her journal, which now included her first visit to California. And she couldn't wait to see what might be in store for them next.

THE END

ABOUT THE AUTHOR

-Author Portrait by Melissa Nolen-

Jamie McGillen lives in the shadow of Mount Rainier, and no matter how many times she moves away, it draws her home. Everything about large evergreen trees delights her, except how poky they are, and the sap.

Her poems and essays have been published in numerous literary journals, and she teaches English Composition at Highline College.

She also loves to chat with readers, so say hello on social media, send her an email, or leave a review and you'll make her day! (Every time you leave a review for this book, a baby book angel gets its wings. Don't deprive them, for heaven's sake.) You can connect and find out more about her at www.jamiemcgillen.com.

instagram.com/jamiemcgillen

facebook.com/jamiemcgillen

BOOK CLUB QUESTIONS

1. In what ways are Anna and Emily different in their aspirations? How are they the same?
2. Which character did you most relate to? Why do you think that is?
3. What were your initial impressions of Emily? How does her character change throughout the story?
4. Anna and Ben read and discuss a number of novels throughout this story. Have you read any of them? If so, did you like them?
5. Have you ever attempted to climb a mountain before? If so, can you relate to anything Anna experienced? If not, have you ever worked toward a big goal, and had to dig deep into yourself to accomplish it?
6. In the foreword to this book, Charlotte Austin discusses the gender gap that exists in mountain climbing. She says, "In 1984, Rosie Andrews wrote that most male climbers raised in traditional

Western culture have 'generally been encouraged to perform physically, problem-solve, take risks while [...] girls are usually more sheltered and protected. Rather than being prepared for independence, [women] learn to expect to play a supporting role, which hinges upon reliance on others.'" How did this truth affect Anna? How does it still affect woman today?

7. If you were making a movie out of this book, who would you cast as Anna?

8. What do you think is next for the characters in the story?

ACKNOWLEDGMENTS

Mom and Dad – Thanks for all the hugs and gold stars. You're the ones I've always wanted to impress the most.

Grandma, Mollie, Caroline, Nikki, Peggy, Mary – Thank you for reading early drafts of this story, and sharing your insights and valuable opinions.

Claire – Thanks for being my author bestie. I couldn't do this without you. One day we'll write that historical romance together.

Charlotte Austin – I'm completely in awe of your accomplishments, and I'm honored that you were willing to assist me in getting the climbing details perfect. The world needs more women like you.

Zee Monodee and Christy Carlyle – Many thanks to both of you for your incredible editing skills. This book would not be the same without your collective insights and suggestions.

Amanda Cuff – I'm grateful for your proofreading prowess. It's amazing how many tiny errors *almost* slip through the cracks.

Scott – I love you more than the raven loves her treasure, and I'm proud of the mature young man that you've become.

Rachel – You are the bestest daughter in the whole wide west! Can you read these words?

MOM

DAD

SCOTT

RACHEL

JAKE

@Laurenbgarcia and @Lauren_loves_cats101 – Thank you both for being sunbeams in an author's world.

Peggy and Linda – Thanks for putting up with me when I was just the weird neighbor kid. I couldn't help but name a couple moms after you guys.

My amazing book launch team: Stefanie, Cara, Katie, Ally, Tristan, Ashley, Ashlee, Lindsay, Trinity, Esmeralda, Hannah, Danielle, Sierra, MaryEllen — How can I thank you all enough? I'm forever grateful for your collective support and enthusiasm.

Made in the USA
Columbia, SC
11 November 2021